I0572328

Anthology 2023

Bayside Writers' Group

Published in Australia
Printed by Ingram Spark

Anthology 2023
Authors: Anne Sedgley, Ann Simic, Di Motton, Ed
Davis, Jacqueline Chevalier Stephens, Jenny Chevalier,
Jess Walters, Joseph Shellim, Judith Dowling, Katherine
Hoffman, Leonie Wells, Lisa Westhaven, Lorraine Doney,
Lucy Tomov, Maxim Anderson, Nathan Clark, Peter Levy,
Rahaf Al Maalouf, Roslyn Evans, Sharon Hurst, Sandra
Lanteri, Zhiling Gao

Design: Sharon Hurst

Acknowledgements

I would like to thank all those who took the effort to submit their works to us.. Several of our regulars have had a challenging year and are not with us, so we look forward to them rejoining our publication next year.

Please note that if anyone would like to make contact with any of the writers in this collection, or would like to be involved in future editions, please email us:

baysidewritersgroup@bigpond.com

Contents

Two faces

He held the car door open for me – that was the first surprise. I climbed in, trying to be graceful.

"I thought we'd have dinner at Two Faces. That all right?"

"Fine", I said. I had heard of Two Faces, a swanky, very expensive restaurant in South Yarra.

I don't like sports cars much. They are too low-slung, so the passenger seat nearly scrapes the road and other cars tower over you. But this was fun. He drove expertly. If I'd known we were going to a restaurant I'd have worn my red leather gloves.

A head-waiter welcomed us and showed us to a table at the back of the dining room.

"Let's start with a gin and tonic," my new friend said. "You like gin and tonic, Anne?"

"I do," I said. "It's the only drink I could have three glasses of in a row."

"Shall I order a couple more for you?" He smiled.

"No, thanks!"

"Here's your menu, then. Let's see whether the food here lives up to its reputation." He chose a seafood entree and fish main course; I played safe with chicken. I'd had dinners where I'd had to battle so hard with my food – finding fishbones or struggling with spatchcock, for example - that I couldn't focus on the conversation. I wanted to get to know this man well. His name was

George Robertson, and he had a lovely expressive face and a beautiful deep voice.

"What do you do, George?"

"I'm a writer. A novelist."

"Have you had any books published?"

"Yes, three so far. The best known is called _Hollow Cave_ – you might have heard of it."

"No, I haven't. But I'll look out for it." I bought it a few weeks later – a tale of shifting perspectives, not grounded - very strange.

He went on: "I've got writer's block at the moment. Not sure what to write about, or what's worth writing about. That's why I put the ad. In the paper. I need to meet more people."

"Have you had other answers to your ad?"

"Yes, I've met several women. All very different from each other, of course. Some were very nice. But not exactly what I need right now. Although it was fun to meet them. What about you?   What do you do?   Are you married? Single? What do you think about Life?"

"Cripes," I said, helped by the G & T. "I'm single and looking around. I would _like_ to be a writer, but I'm not at all self-confident about that, and you do need to be."

He nodded.

"I'm a librarian, and my training was in English Literature and English language. I studied the most abstruse subjects I could find, ones with absolutely no vocational content. Old Icelandic language and literature, for instance."

"Goodness," he said. "Now _that_ sounds interesting. What sort of literature do they have?"

"You know the Icelandic sagas? They tell the stories of the early settlers in Iceland. The sagas are the histories of people with a great oral tradition in prose and in poetry.

The old epic poetry of the Scandinavians is where much of our knowledge of Nordic gods and mythology comes from. Their warriors hope to go to Valhalla, the Hall of the Brave, when they die. And the legends of Odin and Thor and Loki and the giants – they all come from Old Norse cultural traditions."

He asked, "Where do the Vikings fit in?"

"They were Norwegian seafarers who spoke Old Norse, and sailed everywhere, trading with all sorts of cultures and civilizations. They discovered North America, sailing from Iceland up the west coast of Greenland and down past Canada to Newfoundland. There is archaeological evidence of Vikings in all those lands. They traded a lot in the Mediterranean and some joined the emperor's guard in Constantinople. They were pirates, violent, lawless and much feared as fighters. They would go berserk every now and then, killing everything in their path. *Berserk* was the Icelandic word for *Bear's coat*'.

He looked interested. "Did they pull a bear's skin over themselves when they were about to rampage?"

"That's what I've always imagined."

We had an enchanted evening. He questioned me about my family, my friends, my bushwalking, my reading, my job as a librarian. He was an exceptionally good listener, asking questions, resting his eyes on my face in a calm, attentive manner. I have never experienced such interested listening. I told him this: "Most people are waiting until you pause, so they can turn the talk back to themselves." George agreed.

By midnight it was clear that George and I were made for each other. I was too happy and buoyed up to think long-term, but something in me had taken wing, a new internal lightness I had never felt before.

Desserts, coffees and chocolates were behind us now. We'd been the last in the restaurant for an hour. I had no doubt that we would see each other again.

I thanked him for a lovely evening.

"No, no." he'd said. "I'm the one who should thank you. I have had a wonderful night, far better than I'd hoped."

"*Well*, then …" I thought.

We had been parked outside my place for 40 minutes. Perhaps he was shy. I leaned over and kissed him softly on the cheek.

He turned towards me, smiled that beautiful slow smile with his eyes, and leaning across me, pressed the door handle. "Good-night", he said. "I hope all goes well with you. Good luck with the writing."

I stumbled up and out of the low-slung sports car. He waited until I had opened my front door, waved – we both waved – and he drove off. I never saw him again.

I've never seen a book by George Robertson with a character who sounds like me. Tentative, friendly, trusting, gullible, lost in fantasy, and hopeful - ever-hopeful.

Anne Sedgley

2023 response to Judith Wright's poem, *Australia 1970*

Cry beloved country, as you die. Claw back
53 summers — imperilled, exalted eaglehawk, close to
last stand, groping for breath. Cry — boldly protest the
monumental lie.

The tiger snake still hisses its venom,
slithers from all killers on its trail.
It lives and thrives and petrifies me,
as I slink away in awe, and quail.

The ironwood suffers still the clearing chop but hope
lies in our greening days, defying soil's depletion and
erosion at this nth hour, abandoning implosion.

We ply like ants that soldier on,
oblivious to the threats we pose;
we steer a path far, far away
and keep the wretched ants at bay.

We've miles to go to cure our aching earth, to live in
peace with scorpion and snake, to stop self-poisoning,
to eat and have our cake, killing the earth that feeds us.

Drought, fire, tornado and typhoon engulf us — half a
century on, you are still right, as earth unleashes all its
fury, it is our judge, it is our jury.

Ann Simic

Pigs

At the Hotel Gellert. From a terrace facing the Liberty Statue a heroic marble dame holds aloft a branch of palm. Through the arc of the palm I saw a tiny bat flit through the tragic historied spaces of that Budapest night sky. At its poignant hurtle through those love-void spaces punctured by officialdom's towers in the Hungarian sky, I felt for the bat a fearing love.

Then in crept this thought; if I, a biblically irrelevant crumb of a human can love this fleery, despised, little stumbler in the dark, then how much more might the Creator of the universe love it! And if He does, would it be possible that a creature included in God's being could go at its death to oblivion? To nothing?

Now, that'd be batty!

*

So, my vagabond's rattling around starts off in Hungary. I slum on a sofa of the hotel as its TV screen goes on prattling. But its cement flat tone turns in a moral BOOM! The report is of an accident. A gargantuan truck of live-animal transport was on its way to the Miskolc abattoirs. It rolled down a hill, crashed to its side with 300 of its baby pigs, their bones mangled in their iron cages, each and every piglet crushed, squashed to death.

And the driver? Was he impaled? Pierced by a plank? At least skinned alive by slitting glass? Is anything of the driver broken? Dead? In that canon-shot justice of this world, not a scratch! He's just bleary and jokey, blathering barmy stuff to the reporter. Lucky fella!

And now, to the diabolically next!

Onto the screen flashes an ad. It is about how to purchase a pig. On the TV screen it says, you can buy one live, just as advertised, so you can have a little piggy-pet for yourself. The piggy-wiggy can be all yours, tended and coddled for you, so sing-songs the ad. And all the piggy darlings you will ever purchase are promised to be 'well kept'. 'Right until you're ready. When the fattening has reached its time,' purrs on the ad., 'they will be 'processed'. (There it is! That's the ugly sneak of a euphemism hiding the monstrousness, as) that once pampered, darling TV pet of yours shall be stuck, that is, pierced on its neck, stabbed and run through with a blade, to die in screams of an anguish you shall never hear, or suspect, or for a second, ever imagine, it shall be butchered, cosmetically made-up, and its body parts of your own very personal selection shall be immaculately packaged and sent to the dear and respected customer, you. Who may now chose to boil, roast, or pickle it!

There's choice for you!

There's the screen for you!

About as infernal as TV advertising gets.

Katherine Hoffman

Greenpoint

The sea is angry, it bubbles and roars,
The stiff southerly breeze brings tears to our cheeks,
Summer has left us, but seagulls still soar.
Their squarks are a chorus over waves and whitecaps
that peak. A salty spray and a dark sky peppered with
moody clouds,
Herald a weather change with a sky that will leak.

I am Greenpoint that is tested by fickle Port Phillip Bay,
A sentry of time counting the ships that meander every
hour of the day.
With flashing beacons winking on and off. Is it a signal
for wayward vessels on the ley?
Or a call to sea creatures that it is time to play.

I am Brighton Beach of which there are perhaps
another two. One in England. But also, Gallipoli. Oh, but
a few!
The cliffs of Gallipoli seem so far from Greenpoint,
But not so far from the memories of young men who
had a similar view.
Amidst the confusion of a fragmented war that had no
point,

It's a calm sea at Greenpoint with a winter sun on our
backs.
Bringing a new dawn with mottled sky and light through
the cracks.
Not so far from the road traffic beating the lights
without much care.

But oh, so close that the smell of salty air
Is punctuated by diesel and bike riders shouts of 'Don't
be a lair'.

Ed Davis

Grief

Grief is not gentle: it has teeth and claws.

In summer when the sunshine warms your shoulders
It is not dead but sleeping.

In autumn when the leaves are red and dripping
Grief is stirring.

In winter there is emptiness,
Until grief comes howling.

Anne Sedgley

Europe 1977: Train exploits

For me the idea of train travel always conjures romantic visions of the Venice-Simplon Orient Express flying its way through the dark night to Istanbul. Shadowy figures in dark garb move up and down the corridors. Glamorous women, swathed in furs, are followed by porters struggling with mountains of expensive luggage. Intrigue and the possibility of murder lurk somewhere in the train adding another dimension of appeal. Such it is to have read too many Agatha Christie novels.

Many years ago, before upright airline style seats were introduced to European trains, first class train travel meant being able to sit in a six-seat compartment, each with its own wooden panelled sliding door, an entrée into a cosseted world of luxury and contented travel. Most trains had velour or leather seats, quaint white anti-Macassars on the head rests, ornate brass luggage racks and nostalgic sepia photographic scenes of far-flung European cities circa 1910. Some first-class carriages even had their own sitting room with freestanding armchairs and mahogany tables to enhance the travel experience.

In each compartment the window seats were of course the most coveted, not just for the panoramic view they provided, but because each window seat had its own pull-out metal table, ready to place your provisions on, or rest your favourite book. Very civilized. People could sit wherever they felt, provided they had a first-class ticket.

The train conductors savagely evicted any second-class travellers intent on freeloading their way above their status.

Having bought a Eurail pass that entitled us to first-class travel for three months through Europe, husband and I excitedly boarded our first train from Victoria Station in London to speed our way to the Continent. This was to be our first great adventure abroad and every aspect of the train, from the dining car to the toilets, was eagerly inspected; even the signs in French and English were pored over and school girl French dragged from the back of the brain to compare the translations. After a few bruises and humiliating falls in the corridors, our body movements evolved to match the sway of the train.

It took us a few days of travelling to realize that selfishly we preferred a carriage to ourselves. We soon learned how to gain the most benefit from this mode of transport. We always arrived early at the station, ready to pounce on a carriage that was to our liking and one that was empty of other travellers.

Sometimes to our great disappointment, we had to share.

Eventually, through a few heart-to-heart whinges between husband and I, we devised a strategy to eliminate all other passengers from our compartment. Shoes were taken off straight away to reveal smelly socks worn for three or four days, emitting an overpowering aroma. This was the first line of defence for warding off strangers.

The next step in the campaign was to open the tin of sardines we always carried as an emergency ration in the backpack. We opened the tin with great relish, dragged out a baguette and spooned out the oily sardines, mashing them on the bread, their smell filling the compartment. Dropping a few globs on the floor was obligatory. Normally, if we had banished fellow passengers, this food source would have been our last culinary preference to be eaten when all other supplies had run out. Runny French camembert or brie were much more favoured fare, to spread liberally on our baguette, munching our way through the food as the French countryside flashed past.

If the smelly fish failed, there was plan c, the hauling of the wine bottle out of the backpack high up on the luggage rack and having it bounce at the feet of unsuspecting passengers. The prospect though of a breakage was a concern. Then followed the opening of the bottle of red wine, achieved with great straining and grunting sounds from husband, as the cork was finally pulled. Copious amounts of wine would then be poured into our mega sized plastic cups. Spilling some was also a good part of the game plan, though this had to be tempered by the clear desire to avoid too much wastage. Being too friendly could also be an error in behaviour. There was always the possibility that our companions might in fact be latent alcoholics who might decide to ingratiate themselves with us and share our vino.

Desiring to travel overnight on a train to avoid the exorbitant cost of staying in a hotel, we spent many nights at midnight huddled on a semi dark platform waiting for the train to arrive. We would then pounce on an empty carriage, pull down the blinds, spread our belongings out and give greasy looks to anyone who dared to enter our carriage.

On these nights we pulled the seats out and joined them in the middle to create one enormous space, rather like having your own queen size bed on wheels. This proved to be most salubrious when we were on our own. We spread our limbs out over the huge space and using our jumpers as pillows, drifted off to sleep to the rhythmic cachunck,cachunck of the train's motion. On other occasions, when we had not succeeded in removing fellow passengers, we would teach them how to share this extra area, easily accommodating four people lying across the bed. It proved to be a very strange experience lying side by side with total strangers, nodding off to sleep, listening to the murmur of their breathing two inches from your face!

The highlight of one of these nights was when we were heading from Bordeaux to Madrid. We shared the bed with two Spaniards, a man and a woman, who spoke no English. My Spanish was rudimentary at best. We smiled and gestured a little, reserved with each other despite the close quarters. But after the border guards had checked our passports, our fellow passengers proceeded to pull out sweet pastries and chorizo sausage, smiling and entreating us to share their bounty. We retrieved a bottle of wine from our luggage and like naughty school kids at boarding school eating a midnight feast, munched our way through northern Spain, then curled up contentedly next to our new found friends.

I have often wondered what other magic moments we had missed by being anti social for so long.

Di Motton

Waiting

They put me in the oral hygiene room
An hour ago
Beneath the bright pink poster
Of healthy gums.

I've waited for you all over the city
In waiting rooms and pubs and lounges.
Now
They put me in the oral hygiene room.

I watch the different feet go past the door
Through the venetians.
Foot of dental nurse
Foot of dental surgeon.

But no-one comes to ask why I am waiting
Alone and clear and dis-embodied
Here
In the oral hygiene room.

Anne Sedgley

Corporation

As the large 'honey tongued' Head Crow,
master appropriator of other people's ideas,
struts darkly into the Boardroom
he is oblivious of his colleagues' murmurings
and quiet-eyed pretence,
a furtive language they had only recently perfected

so when he closes the meeting
and swaggers imperiously to the exit
his hubris fails to notice
the malicious mirth in their faux deference

he has no idea how people see him
no premonition of what is to come,
how his feathers will be ruthlessly plucked
as he has plucked

and how, in naked exile of denial
he will caw continuously in vain
against those in the unhearing barn yard

Sandra Lanteri

Oy vay! My Muela, my Muela

Oy vay! Is my Muela (grandmother in Spanish) a real character? What she may lack for in tact, she makes up for with presence! My Muela, Regina de Santos de Ferera, has PRESENCE! All four and a half feet tall of her.

Her Spanish ancestry, of the wealthy and powerful de Ferera family, gives her the fire, determination, emotional intensity and pride which sparkles in her eyes and gives her rotund little figure strength and dignity. Her Jewish roots have endowed her with some distinctive qualities which epitomize the typical Jewish mother, or 'Yiddish Mama': hypersensitivity, a master of emotional manipulation, an eardrum shattering voice, extreme insecurity, bordering on paranoia, and a Freudian obsession with food. She is also playful, adventurous, irresistibly unabashed in expressing herself and has a fantastic and earthy sense of humour.

However, her vulnerable side has been seen by few. At night, in the cover of darkness, her hair trapped in curlers and scarf, she discards her day-face to confront yet another night of aloneness, since her mate's death some years ago.

She often wakes, whimpering in her sweaty sheets, from the doubts and fears which parade in the grotesque garb of nightmares, sending her strong hand scurrying, shakingly, under her pillow to grasp some solace and comfort from the old leatherbound book of Hebrew prayers. This vulnerable side has contributed to her mouth's appearance of an old scar, stitched into taut, quiet suffering.

This lonely side has given her honey-coloured eyes a misty fermented expression. The demanding, and at times, overbearing character of my Muela, leaves me often bemused and frustrated, with my palms and eyes raised to the sky. And yet, when I am ill and she comes to me, her eyes full of love, and in her hands a bowl of steaming hot chicken soup: "for my little Elizabetha", I am humbled, and thank God for this quirky Muela of mine.

Jacqueline Chevalier Stephens

Knotweed

practising is a hollowed out fallacy
how must I uproot
unpetal
sprout in a teacup;
there is little earth in porcelain
bone dry
bone yellow
misaligned
what is that all below?
talking to my roots.

Lucy Tomov

A hindranced cell

In the freezing squeeze of a jungle thicket
There appeared, what one might call,
A hindranced cell

Which, mind you, was really due
To that same reflection
Often un-clever
But never once commonly un-hearty

Now the cell too didn't always carry its expected
measure
And, although this won't deter one growing fondness
Bear in mind please
Even in the truest reflection of a sure but shy promise
There can emerge
That sudden, but un-called for, squeeze
That can freeze the very essence of a melting pot.

Joseph Shellim

True love came to me

True love came to me, where with another I boldly
stood,
And a different man may have taken both
And be one lover, long I stood
And looked into one as far as I could
To where her body moved in right places;

Then chose Sharon, as just as fair,
And having perhaps the better claim,
Because she was loving and knew what I should wear;
My jeans and jocks so faded here and there
I'd worn them really about the same,

And both that morning equally lay
On my Newstead Rd bed on my sack.
Oh, did I keep the old ones for another day?
No! Yet knowing how way leads on to way,
I realized my life would never go back.

I shall be telling this with a wryness
Somewhere ages and ages hence:
True love emerged in front of me, and I,
I took Sharon,
And that has made all the difference.

Peter Levy (with apologies to Robert Frost)

Brighton, where we live

Today, as I very often do, am enjoying my cappuccino at the Dendy Baths Cafe overlooking our wonderful sandy beach. The weather today is 25 degrees. A light breeze caresses my face. I have just finished my exercises at the gym, had my swim and sauna and now, bliss, am enjoying my favourite latte.

I am just thinking what restaurant will I book for this evening? There are so many to choose from in Brighton: Will we eat Italian, Thai, or maybe Indian before going to the Bay Cinema to watch one of the French Festival films? It is Sunday and this afternoon after lunch at the Deli I will pop over to my supermarket to do some shopping. What will we do without our great supermarkets today? The range of vegetables, fruit, the variety of cheeses, all the delicacies displayed, some from local and imported sources, to enjoy these days. Well, I must say that we are really spoiled here as we lack for nothing nowadays.

Brighton known as a "charming little village" with its elegant boutiques, displays the latest fashion from Australia and overseas.

Brighton can boast beautiful sandy beaches that compare very nicely with some of the best beaches in the world. The iconic bathing boxes on Brighton beach are so colourful. They date back about 50 years.

The best place to enjoy a swim is of course at the Brighton Baths. They were built in 1881 as a centre of

Recreation. Today, they are some of the only caged open-water sea baths in Australia'.

The facilities at the Brighton Baths include 50 meters lap lanes, a steam room overlooking Port Phillip Bay and the state of the art gym. The club is also home to the Brighton Sea Baths Icebergers, a passionate community of swimmers who use the pool all year round.

The Royal Brighton Yacht Club, a few hundred meters away, has, been developed today to include a cafe/restaurant and several new amenities where you can meet people of all nationalities speaking many different languages.

The Billila Mansion is another beautiful land-mark. My daughter Jacquie got married at Billila, This historical mansion was built in 1878.

Bayside and indeed Brighton was nothing like it is today when we arrived by ship at Port Melbourne in the early fifties. We had decided to come to Australia as we were keen to explore parts of the world and also because my aunty and my English uncle had settled there a couple of years before and encouraged us to join them there saying that we would love to live there as there were a lot of opportunities for us young people, that life in Melbourne was very pleasant and Australians were very friendly people.

On arrival, both my aunty and uncle picked us up. We took a taxi to their home. On the way, looking out the window, my husband and I were surprised to notice how deserted the streets were. It was early in the day and not a soul to be seen.

"Where is everybody," I asked?

"It's Sunday dear. Everything is closed and most people tend to their garden, wash their cars or are at church."

'Oh!" I said, very surprised. A far cry from where we came from.

There were no cafes, restaurants or any venues as we know today, only milk bars and pubs! I remember putting on a lot of weight by trying milk shakes, fish and chips wrapped in newspapers and of course the traditional meat pies.

My husband and I missed sitting in a cafe like today, or having a meal in a restaurant with friends. Going to see a play, or a concert. The Arts Centre and Concert Hall did not exist then.

A few years ago, I saw a short film recounting the story of the very first coffee shop that opened in very Victorian Melbourne.

The owner, an Italian, missed so much his cup of coffee on arrival in Australia that he decided to import the first espresso machine from Italy. It took a long time when it finally arrived by ship to Melbourne. In the meantime, he had found a venue in the city with the intention of opening his first coffee shop in Melbourne. (We had to be content where we lived with a make- believe coffee of chicory.)

There was a great celebration that day at the coffee shop. All his friends were invited, including the local priest. Expectations were high. They were finally going to sip the first cup of their favourite brew, they missed so much.

"Who will savour the first cup?" asked the wife. "We should offer it to our priest of course."

'No way!" said Mr Pelligrini. "The first cup will be for me! I waited long enough, Sorry Father."

It's on this day that the first coffee shop in Melbourne was finally born.

It took several years for us in Brighton and indeed to all of Bayside to be able to enjoy our first brew in our own coffee shop.

The food variety was very slim. Fruit shops mainly

offered huge carrots, huge zucchinis, potatoes and peas. A staple at the time. There were not many varieties in fruit either. On the other hand, the meat, especially the lamb was top quality. I did enjoy a good leg of lamb for Sunday lunch which my uncle always sliced and served to us all with roast potatoes and peas.

I remember one day my aunty saying. "Today I prepared a stuffed zucchini for lunch. I think you will enjoy it.

"One zucchini?" I asked "For the whole family?"

"Wait till you see the size of it," she replied.

Brighton was completely deserted in the evening, everyone stayed at home as there was no where to go.

Another thing was that if we happened to speak French on the tramway or even in the streets, we were given dirty looks.

"Why don't you speak English? You are in Australia now!"

I guess that Australians being so isolated from the rest of the world were not ready to accept "New Australians" as we were called.

As I mentioned before, I found Australians were quite laid-back in their daily life.

I also had trouble understanding the Australian accent and vernacular as it was much stronger than the way it is today. Some of these expressions which come to mind were "My word!" "She's apples mate" a "sheila" (a girl) and some others I can no longer recall as they are quite passe today.

An English lady was sick in hospital and needed help. She rang the nurse several times to no avail.

When the nurse finally turned up, the lady said to her, "Oh, there you are! You certainly took your time. Did I come here to die?"

"No, you came here yesterday," replied the nurse.

Yes, things were so different in those days. We were really disappointed and bored living in Brighton to the point that my husband and I wished we could return home. This was however quite impossible for us as firstly we did not have enough money for the trip and facing another 30 days aboard a ship was out of the question. Mind you we definitely do not regret not having left then.

In desperation, I and a friend of mine whose father was a carpenter, decided to draw plans to rent a venue with an outdoor area to start a cafe/bistro in Church Street. I approached the Brighton Council with our plans.

"I love the idea,"he said, but they will never accept it, the reason given is that's a very "unhealthy" proposition!"

"Well, no-one has died just by going to a cafe all over Europe and indeed the world, that I know of!" I said.

In those days, many were reluctant to change. Everything had to remain the same. I guess it took a long time for people to finally accept that we really had to advance and join the rest of the modern world.

It was interesting to learn some of the history of Bayside and especially Brighton's, as indeed Brighton and Bayside have a colourful history.

I t took two petitions for the government to proclaim the Municipality of Brighton, in 1858. Later Brighton grew and was proclaimed a Borough in 1863, then later a city. The names of Bayside reflect this colourful history. Its streets, beaches and parkland are named after the early pioneers who braved the unknown and contributed to Bayside growth.

The people of the stone

300 years ago, the Ngaruk Willam clan of the Boon Wurrung people lived on the land from Brighton to Mordialloc. Three foreshore sculptures at North Road, Red Bluff & Ricketts Point can still be found along the coastal trail and foreshore.

The first lands development in Brighton began in 1841 when the Government sold parcels of land. The land sold offered no more than a wilderness edged by beautiful beaches.

Henry Dendy, on his arrival in Melbourne bought 5120 acres. He bounded his extensive property with the roads that still exist today: North, South and East Boundary Roads.

Dendy through the depression died poor. His name, however lives on: Dendy Street, Dendy Park, Dendy Village, Dendy Beach and even the Dendy cinema.

Another perhaps, the most well-known Bayside figure of the 19th was Sir Thomas Bent who from a Market gardener became Premier of Victoria in (1904 - 1909). He is remembered in Bentleigh and Bent Parade in Black Rock. A Statue of his stands over the corner of Bay Street and Nepean Highway Brighton.

In the early days Bayside attracted the wealthy who erected beautiful mansions. Some of these grand estates are still here. "Castlefield, on the corner of South Road and Hampton Street, lives on as a part of Haileybury College in South Road. Another grand manor is visible at the Sandringham Club.

Another area commemorates a famous local event in 1924. Two men held up the Hampton branch of the Commercial Bank of Australia and shot 22-year-old William Almeida who despite his wound gave chase and brought one of the men back to the bank at gun point. The next day Almeida died of his injuries. 22-year-old William Almeida is honoured by a drinking fountain in the Triangle Garden on the corner of Linacre and Hampton Streets in Brighton.

We have lived in Brighton all these years and had a chance to witness all the changes that happened during our stay. We now feel very lucky, my family and I to be part of Brighton. A modern and great sea-side suburb to live in.

Jenny Chevalier

The little knight

He wore his shield.
He carried his sword.
The little knight in the battle was called.

Stepping forward was harsh.
Yet, staying back was harsher.
He gathered his strength to march.
What a warrior, what an archer.

Suddenly, the little knight fell to the ground.
His strength let him down in the round.
What a betrayal, what a decay.
How can this huge power leave him and go away?

He decided to give up, he decided to surrender.
He abandoned his sword, and waited for the murderer.

Unexpectedly, a flash of golden lights came from the
sky.
Went through his body and lifted his energy high.

Those lights gave him a spear to fight and wings to fly.
Eventually, he won the battle and breathed a relieved
sigh.

Rahaf Al Maalouf

Corned beef by the bay

Each year since her only child Faye was fifteen Bea Baxter had packed her off to bayside Brighton for the summer to stay with her Aunt Muriel and Uncle Keith at 'Dalkeith' their gracious beach-front home.

Muriel and Keith were childless and it had been long decided by them that Faye, being their only sane relative within cooee, would inherit 'Dalkeith' and all the chattels that came with it. This wasn't exactly spoken of but the widowed Bea desperately wanted it to be the case, and she did all she could to ensure that Faye endear herself to her brother-in-law and her sister.

So there we have 25-year-old Faye in 1962, basking in the sun and shallows of the beach at Brighton where, at that time, sixty eight bathing boxes stood spread out along the sand following the curve of the foreshore, parallel to the gentle swoop of the road as it meanders through Melbourne's bayside suburbs.

Mooralong, where Faye had grown up was by contrast just a speck of a township in eastern New South Wales. There Faye had spent her childhood, apart from a brief and unsuccessful sojourn at boarding school which was provided by her Uncle Keith in an effort to counteract the disinterest her widowed mother had in the value of education for girls. Hence on her fourteenth birthday Faye took her position as mother's companion whilst awaiting arrival of a suitor.

Faye positioned herself in front of a bathing box feeling strangely independent. She had spent many an hour perusing order catalogues for the latest in beach wear. She was pleased with her elasticised bathers with built-in bra, she loved her yellow spotted towelling beach jacket with matching tote carry-all, and her Chinese coolie hat. She had also dared to send away for a 'Pearly Plush Pink' lipstick and nail polish and even an attractive blue rubber bathing cap covered in white rubber daisies. Indeed, she felt she was a true 60s beach girl.

A young man, who she was soon to know as Kelvin, appeared from between two bathing boxes stepping through an assortment of trodden-down coastal grasses. He sat on the step of a bathing box which immediately gave-way.

"Jesus! What the hell!" he shouted as he tried to keep himself upright. He moved closer to where Faye was sitting.

"Sorry about the language," he said. "Half these boxes are sub-standard. Public safety problems. The council couldn't care less. Some people say these places will be worth big money in a few years and they'll be a huge tourist attraction when they're all done up. It'll never happen but then some people have more money than sense. That's what I say."

Kelvin repositioned himself nearer to Faye. He lit a cigarette and made perfect smoke rings.

"Honestly this place stinks of dog piss," he said, with his thumb indicating the area at the back of the bathing boxes. "Dogs on beaches! It ought to be made illegal. Sooner the better I say."

Faye frowned and waved cigarette smoke from her

vicinity. "I really wish they'd ban cigarettes on beaches," she said.

"Nah, That'll never happen. No way. Coming for a dip? Watch out for sharks. Did you know that way back in the thirties a person dived off the pier straight into the mouth of a shark. I hear there was quite a trail of blood," he laughed as he pointed out the pier not far up the beach on the right.

"I've got to go. I've got to catch the butcher for the corned beef for dinner. It closes dead on 12noon on Saturday," Faye said as she brushed sand from her legs then headed to the roadway.

"I wish the day would come when you can shop any time of day or night. What do ya think?" she said.

"Ridiculous idea Faye. Nah that won't happen." Kelvin called. "Hey, did I hear you say corned beef? For dinner? Carrots, parsnip, parsley, buttery white sauce? It's my absolute favourite! Please invite me. If you do I'll adore you for ever. Watch the road now! There should be traffic lights there. Mark my words its gunna be a traffic nightmare around here before long. In a few years you'll have to pay dollars to have a swim."

Earlier in the day Aunt Muriel had called out to Faye, "We'll have corned beef for tea. Ok Faye? Would you pop into the butcher's after your swim? I won't be able to get there myself - I've got the bridge girls coming at 2 and I'd better make a sponge."

Muriel called out as Faye walked out the front door.

"Ah good," chimed in Uncle Keith. "Corned beef for dinner! You just have to throw a nice h-bone end into a big pot with a few cloves added and boil hell out of it for about three hours. Then like magic, some man will become infatuated with you and your extraordinary culinary powers. Trouble is we all change and before you know it every second one of us will not allow meat anywhere near the kitchen. It's a sad state of affairs. Mark my words, we'll be eating nothing but very peculiar looking raw vegetables in a few years. Can you imagine life without a nice lamb chop or a rasher of bacon? Perish the thought!"

Muriel shuddered, "Keith! Oh Keith, we'll all be dead if that happens.'

So now my Poppet it's 1982 and corned beef's slipped right off the menu. Aunt Muriel's in a nursing home overlooking the bay. She was watching the news of the first shark attack in Port Philip Bay sixty years ago and when she jumped up and told the room full of 'friends' that she remembered the original event.

"Muriel," her best friend said, "You've lost the plot." The nurses gave her three extra tablets and put her to bed.

Kelvin came out proudly gay with the best partner a man could have. They are planning their wedding day though it's all just a pipe dream - Kelvin knows it'll never happen ..... then again who knows? You never know what the future will bring.

Look at Bea. She went back to school at seventy-five and is now the mayor of Mooralong, holding garden parties for Women's Rights and happy hours.

Things happen. Brighton has nine new bathing boxes and their owners are taking much more pride in them these days, in fact 'They' say that by the year 2000 they will be selling for $30,000 .... ridiculous I know, but then again, who knows? Faye unfortunately didn't play her cards right and therefore doesn't reside in the bay area. She recently gave birth to her second set of twins. It was all due to this amazing new artificial insemination program that people only whispered about a few years ago. Now it's something you can pop out for in your lunch hour. No detailed news has come to hand but it is general knowledge that a genuine 60's Chinese coolie hat sold for $26,000 on 'BigDeal' not long ago. Faye's 1960's bathers perished in the seventies and were rejected by the Salvos.

In the twenty years since 1962, Kelvin still fondly remembers the dinner at 'Dalkeith'. The corn beef was just right. It simply fell off the fork just as it was supposed to.

There are some things that never change! The Keep Corned Beef Alive Fan Club members meet up and eat up at various homes and restaurants in the bayside area. Membership is mainly men but women are most welcome. This is just one of the many innovative initiatives of our outstanding community.

Judith Dowling

Meeting place

I leave loneliness in an empty house
Of late winter lockdown,
Drive to the outer limits of our prescribed boundaries
To walk through gate of Long Hollow Heathland.
Reserve Road's car exhaust, traffic noise
Give way to wrens' chirps, frogs' glug-glug,
Whispers in branches above.
I head to wooden walkway
Above damp swamp.
A colourful sign board catches my eye.
A shard of recognition strikes my body.
I twirl around, silently shout with surprise:
"My great, great grandparents are here with me!"

I read the information board again more carefully:
"Early settlers James and Susannah Moysey recorded
the earliest descriptions
Of the vegetation in Black Rock, Beaumaris, Cheltenham
and Mentone in 1844".
With Susannah's fresh gaze I turn to slowly share her
delight
In small balls of cream and vivid yellow wattle.
I follow creeping mistletoe along fence line.
I hear my great great grandmother's voice calling me
across the decades:
"The land was lightly wooded with gum and wattle
trees.
Heath predominated among the native grasses.
And in springtime the place was beautiful with
wildflowers",
Her diary records.

I walk further along sandy track.
Shy Nodding Green Orchids among the grasses
Give way to sea of purple Chocolate Lilies.
Elegant Trigger plants invite my touch,
While Milkmaid's Purse demurely hides behind the
Drooping Sheoak.
I breathe in fragrance.

Thankyou, great great grandmother, for your rich
legacy.

Susannah, I only ever encountered you once before.
When in 1964, as teenager in formal hat and gloves,
I joined my family with father, George Moysey Wilson,
At the solemn clan gathering
Unveiling plaque on the Memorial Cairn, Beach Road.
I traced your name on brass plate.
Hammered to stone edifice.
Below: "Spot of the home of the first white settlers of
this locality."
You would have gazed through small window of your
wattle and daub cottage,
Seen changing colours of sea,
Heard screech of cockies, smelt salt spray on the south
easterly,
Walked along sandy beach, marvelled at middens
hidden by rocks.
Records say you rode boundary fences at night
To check on sheep raids from the Boon Wurrung people
When gold lured James north for a period, leaving you
with small children.

I have mused at what your colonising cost original
inhabitants.

I now have met your two selves:
Your eloquent appreciation of your new natural world,
Your callow dispossession of the first settlers.
My pride, my guilt.
Irreconcilable.

I return to my empty house
Grounded, with an uneasy peace.

Roslyn Evans

Highgate

I am standing in the street opposite number five Inner Crescent where I once lived. It's different now of course, that was over thirty years ago. The old brick fence has been replaced by a picket fence and the garden is no longer a mass of giant Azalea bushes and ancient Camellia trees. The row of hydrangeas that once billowed out along the side of the house are now long gone. I remember watching Granny stand awkwardly on an old wooden crate as she reached up to pick them.

In those days, long before I came to live there, the house was divided in two.

Granny lived on one side and my mother in law along with her husband and two sons lived on the other side. Originally, it had been an old Victorian mansion but was split down the middle to accommodate everyone. It underwent a drastic renovation in the early fifties, modernising the kitchens and bathrooms so that it became two single dwellings. The ceiling roses and cornice were removed, the sash windows replaced with metal ones and the fireplaces upgraded with oil burners and electric radiators. The polished floorboards were covered with swirls of pink and grey floral carpet and the Victorian light fittings were discarded for fifties style chandeliers and wall scones. The old return veranda with its magnificent cast iron lace work was taken off to the tip and the tessellated tiles on the porch were ripped up and replaced with multi coloured crazy stone. The old hawthorn bricks were painted white and a low brick fence replaced the old cast iron one. Only the stained glass front door remained untouched. It was the only evidence that the house had once been Victorian.

The property fanned out, narrow at the front and wide at the back. All show at the front then spreading out into a rabbit warren of outhouses at the back. The rear of the house was a series of partially dilapidated wooden sheds with a large carport, big enough for several cars and a trailer. The carport had a corrugated iron roof with a concrete floor that was reminiscent of a skating rink. A gigantic Cyprus hedge ran along the length of the back fence where the boys used to build cubby houses and play soldiers when they were little until the day they set it on fire.

Fire engines, sirens blaring raced up the laneway that ran between the houses of Inner Crescent and Middle Crescent. They extinguished the flames but the old hedge was left burnt and charred, never to be the same again. My mother-in-law decided the boys needed to be taught a lesson, so they were carted off to the Orphanage in Wilson Street, along with their little suitcases, and left quivering at the front door. Fortunately the orphanage was full, so they were told, and they were allowed to go home as long as they promised never to play with matches again.

In the summer, my mother-in-law would spend the mornings on the beach. She pushed the toddler in the pram along Bay Street all the way down to the beach at Sandown Street. They stayed all morning then came home for lunch and a nap, and went back again in the afternoon. She went day after day, there was no thought of shade or sunscreen, just endless days of sun, sand, and splashing about in the water.

They were the days of mink stoles and Ball Room dancing, of Dinner parties and golf club functions, of off the shoulder dresses, stiletto heels and short permed

Hair, of weekends spent down at Portsea, and nights playing Bridge, and watching movies.

During the sixties things happened that was to alter their way of life forever. My father-law died suddenly which changed everything. The boys finished school and went onto university while my mother-in-law struggled to run the family businesses. She comforted herself with breeding Doberman dogs and won prizes showing them. She took up China painting and painted vases of flowers and scenes of Paris and Rome from her travels overseas. She spent money on fancy clothes and fur coats. She bought herself a Mercedes and after some considerable time found a new companion.

It was made difficult when he came to visit by the fact that Granny did not approve of him. On one occasion when she was outside in the garden watering she turned the hose on him. In the end my mother-in-law moved down to her house at Portsea and divided the property in Brighton in two by having a fence erected down the middle, which resulted in them never speaking again.

Over the years the house began to deteriorate. The paint peeled from the walls the garden grew up between the cracks in the path and everything looked tired and dated. The hedge at the rear of the property grew out of control and became a fire hazard. A neighbour who climbed on the back fence to complain was told to go to hell and then drenched with the garden hose. As he tried to climb down his jumper snagged on the fence and Granny held the hose on him till he was soaked to the bone and his shoes were filled with water.

In the winter the house was cold and damp so Granny decided to move to Girawheen in Outer Crescent for the winter months. As always she did everything independently, packing her jeep with a suitcase and walking there all by herself. In the afternoons she would walk back to Inner Crescent and sit in the front room looking out over the garden or playing solo with her friends. Every Friday she took her walking stick and headed off down Wilson Street to Khyatt's Pub for a counter lunch and a glass of sherry. All at the young age of ninety-six.

One day I went to visit her while she was there during the day. We were sitting in the front room with the sun streaming in through the sheer dusty curtains. She was starting to look frail so I asked her if she was ever afraid of being there at night that someone could break in. She said in all the years she lived there only once had someone tried to break in. She said she just tapped really loudly on the window with her walking stick and told them to bugger off. Apparently they got the fright of their lives, and ran off down the street and she went back to bed. Why didn't you ring the police? Why would I bother doing that she said they had already gone!

The carpets were starting to look threadbare, the paint was peeling from the walls and the curtains harboured years of accumulated dust. It was becoming evident that Granny could no longer look after the house so she moved to Girawheen permanently. The house stood vacant for months on end until it was decided that it was to be sold. At the time we were thinking of moving to a bigger home and it was suggested that we could buy Inner Crescent. It threw up many doubts especially for my husband who would have to contemplate returning to live in the house where he grew up. In the end we made the decision to buy it and set about the mammoth task of restoring it.

We moved in the middle of winter with a new baby and a two year old and no heating except for the oil burner in the lounge room and a strip heater in the bathroom. The first thing we did was open up the door at the end of the hallway, which led into the kitchen. All of a sudden the house was double the size. One side was fifties and the other side where Granny had lived was almost still Victorian and in dire need of renovating.

In the years that followed we slowly put back all the Victorian features. The ceiling roses, cornice, wide skirting boards were all returned to their original state. The fireplaces were opened up and white marble mantelpieces were reinstated. All the carpets were lifted up and the floorboards were repaired and polished. The front windows were returned to their original state and French doors replaced the fifties windows in the dining room. The return veranda, with its cast iron lace work, was reconstructed across the front of the house and down the side. Eventually, all the outhouses and old sheds were demolished.

The front four rooms would be all that remained of the original house. The back of the house that was like a rabbit warren was gone. The new addition was really like a complete home in itself with a kitchen and family room and four bedrooms and two bathrooms. The endless years of renovation were coming to an end.

It was something Granny could never fathom. Why would you want to make it into one big place when you could live in one side and rent the other? The tower at the end of the return veranda had a staircase that led to the upstairs bedrooms and a view across the bay.

After Granny passed away, in her hundredth year, the

front rooms of the house were prone to the groans and creaks that old homes seem to have, but it was the staircase in the tower where the footsteps were heard late at night. Unfortunately it was usually the babysitters that seemed to be spooked by it all. They all told the same story. Once the children had gone to bed they would hear footsteps in the tower upstairs but when they went to check if they were out of bed walking around they would find them sound asleep.

The house was named HIGHGATE after the area Granny came from in London. We lived there until the early nineties, then we went our separate ways, fleeing from the place that bound us, one generation after another, altogether in a world that now belongs to another time.

Leonie Wells

The Japanese artist

We have watched him
painting on Florence's Ponte Vecchio
over many years

we have seen him age, as we have aged
a familiar foreign face
belonging to this city of artists
by his fine aesthetic, and exquisite design,
such a welcome antidote
to the nauseous gold

his wordless presence
formed a visual part of our daily lives-
the pleasure of expectation
the comfort of ritual
our common universal endurance
to keep on keeping on

we always meant to acknowledge his talent
to purchase a painting,
I'm sure you know the feeling,
but we were complacent with the familiar
perhaps arrogant
perhaps naïve
in our false surety of an unchanging tomorrow

therefore words, actions,
were not said, not taken
until the day,
as you have probably surmised,
when he was not there

Our daily visual ritual has now changed
along with the hope he will return,
yet in our minds we see him still,
a double-edged sword this-
our comfort
our regret

Sandra Lanteri

Tilly

applejack cargo pants
flexing hands while choosing midnight snacks
midnight in the window's reflection
midnight in your mouth
the morning we spend unfolding terracotta pots
you looked at me in dappled light
crisp snow green in the backyard
and I remember
a yellow lamp bathed in half questions
would you hold it against me?
would you?
if I memorised every word you said.

Lucy Tomov

I got a song

I got a song where the words are not sung
Where the tune is not played by any band
I sing within my heart of peaceful forgiveness
Of freedom for all in this land.

I got a song where my teardrops keep beat
Where the aim of the melody is to bless
As I sing to you, my oppressor, I weep
For love and understanding those in stress.

I got a song where harmony is in the world
Where brotherhood is accepted by all
I sing with hope in my heart and on my lips
That you will sing too and stand tall.

I got a song . . . I got a song . . . for you.

Peter Levy

Crows

I cannot imagine – have never seen – a baby crow.
I picture it as a tiny ball of black, creaking beyond its
size.
Crows are the avian version of black pine cones
Lying along the topmost branches.

In ancient times, five crows wheeling across the sky
Signified whatever the augurs said they foretold,
Black letters against a bright blue summer sky
Above the golden wheat, the rich brown mould.

In winter in the alps crows pick at the white snow
With long successful beaks. Their yellow eyes
Have seen some shred of offal from far off.
Their angled legs are sticks, their feet are cruel.

Crows on the snow in academic gowns
Strut and deliver peremptory raucous cries:
"Look out!" "This piece is mine!" "My feet are cold!"
Their beaks fill up their faces; they look old.

Crows do not fly like geese in skeins
Draped loosely over quarter of the sky.
They don't adopt the V-formation of ducks
Or the graceful bright white glide of pelicans.

Crows tumble and drift, like scraps of blackened rags
That float above bare paddocks after fire.
They strut and flap, black on a silver bough
And croaking, tell each other they have power.

Anne Sedgley

crack

I like the way you write, which means I like the way you think – that's how it started. An innocent message, kindness itself – just a few words on my screen. I'd been publishing online for years, and this wasn't the first time someone had told me they admired my writing, but from that very first message somehow this was different. No one else has ever said they like the way I think, not even me.

I replied in a few words – something noncommittal and vaguely distant, but I was flattered, of course I was. I didn't entirely realise then from the very first, but he'd already found my weak spot, my vanity, and taken a crowbar to my carapace. His name was Marek, I learned later, but from the beginning I called him bacon man. Why? Because he sizzled.

He liked the way I think. Can I tell you a not-so-secret secret? I think a lot – it's basically a hobby, a competitive sport, if you will. And soon I was thinking a lot about him. Drafting sentence after sentence, holding him in my thoughts during the day, narrating to him my sleepless nights as I tossed and, sometimes, turned. He became my constant companion, my imaginary friend with benefits. I loved holding him inside me. It was company.

Who was it, do you think, who first decided that phones set to stealthy mode should vibrate? Soon after that first back and forth I gave him my number and I began carrying my phone in my trouser pocket, hanging out for the notification. When casually promising to call someone we say, 'I'll give you a buzz', don't we? He gave me a buzz all right, I began to live for it. You're thinking, so soon? Yes, so soon. And I quite agree, this was me at my most pathetic. However, that's the thing when life is a tedious set of duties and requirements – it takes very little to sweep you off your feet. I was craving something, not knowing what it was, and then he came along and suddenly the world was full of light. And, let me tell you, to begin with at least, the pocket vibrations were more than good.

I know, you look at me, your eyebrows firmly embedded in your hairline. What am I? Middle-aged, suited and booted, polished within an inch of my life with a Windsor knot at my neck. You look at me and you think surely not. Surely, this fastidious dry old stick isn't the stupid sort who would throw their life away to chase some destructive love affair, some illicit high – you'd be wrong, of course. You might not be able to tell, actually I hope you can't because I have a persona to maintain, but I've never seen a cliff I didn't want to jump off. Let me tell you, just this once while we are baring souls, any and all emergency exits sing siren songs to me. Can I admit that I often look at oncoming trains with a sense of longing? Destruction is exciting. Burn it all to the fucking ground and while you're at it please, I beg you, use me for kindling.

He liked the way I write. Within just a few days I was in far over my head and I knew it, but that was part of the fatal attraction. We dared each other to be raw and frank – no, let me rephrase that – he dared me, and I willingly stripped myself down to sinew and bone. I have never had a dare I didn't more than meet. Have you ever worked a pole? I'd like to. I see the attraction. Spin and hold, strong and upside down for the gratification and admiration of others. It seems like it would be very pleasing. It's the simple things, right?

Each day and, more so, each night, the stakes were raised. Marek was good at communicating his desire, crude and profound – the two intoxicatingly interchangeable. Who doesn't want to be drowned in another person's need? That's the addictive thing about drowning, right? The euphoria as oxygen becomes a scarce commodity. Did I sometimes do him the favour of adding some finesse, maybe. I sometimes wrote his parts for him as an act of service to our shared desire.

Did I mention he was married? Of course, he was. He'd never had feelings like this before, but he liked the way I write. He read every word and felt like he'd already been inside me. That's what he texted. We agreed, later, he meant inhabited me, though I think his mind, like yours, I can tell from your face, was in the gutter when he wrote it. It was a 2am buzz, I remember. Thinking on it now, likely he was drunk. I'll be honest with you; he was often drunk. Or going out for a smoke break. Sometimes those smoke breaks lasted for days. I never enquired what it was he smoked; I didn't want to know my pocket boyfriend was a junkie when we were both invested in him being to some very large degree straight. Yes, I was a very different person in those days.

Abusers, I've read, start with love bombing and then return to it much later as a strategy to excuse the abuse. The days when he disappeared, melted into silence, felt like weeks – once, checking for the hundredth time, my phone slipped out of my hand and the screen fractured against the floor.

Then there were literal years where he was absent, but I

held an eternal flame. And then each time he came back, like a fucking boomerang hitting me square in the skull. He said I felt like home to him in a hundred different ways he'd never known before. Well, I'm nothing if not accommodating.

Was I playing an adult's high-stakes poker or a childish game of chicken? Both, probably – gambling with my life, willing to lose it all. I'd heard about limerence before, but never experienced it. Not like this. It's described as a bad thing, right? Obsessive, intrusive, delusional, painful. Let me tell you – limerence makes you feel electric. Alive, alive-oh. I loved the waves of shocking joy that hit me each time a new message arrived. Devouring his words, consuming meaning, feeling my palms sweat and my heart beat faster. A masochist to my very marrow, I also enjoyed the downs - when empty silence was all that sat in my pocket. Throughout it all, I knew, in ways I hadn't felt for years, that I was alive.

The mad thing is the music. That's what I miss most when I'm back in the Sahara of absent desire. The way music sounds so fucking meaningful when you're in a limerent high. It's the sound of recaptured youth, right? When the key changes from major to minor or when the beat finally drops. The way it soars and takes you with it. It was easily the biggest gift he ever gave me: Marek made music sound meaningful again. I'd clamp my headphones around my skull and close my eyes. Swooping, soaring – untethered from reality. I always want to feel more than all the feels; please let the bass break me apart. God, now I think of it I pity the people sitting next to me on the metro. There were many days when I cried, silent and still.

What else? The world was brighter. Technicolour gets a bad rap, but let me tell you any kind of wonderland is an amazing place to be. Who wouldn't want to be Alice, growing and shrinking as required? I really enjoyed the acid saturation of thinking someone loved me for the worst parts of me, the way I think, of course I did.

Did the word love surprise you? It's profoundly unwise, isn't it? I fucking loved everything being with, behind the screen, Marek did to me. Yes, okay. Fine. It was, for months on end, simply just a peep hole through which he watched me fuck myself over and over again, you called it. We were never together in any meaningful sense, except that one time.

Astonished? You shouldn't be. We met up once, when the plausible deniability outweighed, just, the co-dependence. It was a strange day – full of tension and discomfort. It's not a case of never meet your heroes, rather never dispel your dreams. Is it shallow of me to judge his footwear? Trainers, not even fashionable ones. Be fair, that finely tuned disgust is sometimes the only thing that's kept me on dry land in the intervening decade.

He was dull, frankly. Bumbling. A rube. The man of my dreams he was not, but I'm a forgiving soul. I think we could have made it work. After hours of staring at each other across a small table in a dark bar, I suggested we kiss.

You wouldn't guess from looking, but I'm a brutal kisser. I will hold you down, hard. Try to come up for air, just try, and I will eat you up. My hips will grind you into the ground. My weight, pushing into and against you will ensure you are held where I want you. And, after having held him hard next to me and found him wanting, the worst thing is I still want him.

I write, I think. I still chase whatever smack I wish he would give me and hate myself for even just slightly holding out for him. I wish we'd fucked, just once. It would have been disappointingly bad sex, an exorcism. Don't tell me otherwise, because I already lie to myself all too often. Here's an essential truth: nobody in muddy runners has ever made me come, I know this. And, yet, he inhabits my dreams.

How do you dry out? Have you ever tried? I like to swap one addiction for another – a change is as good as a holiday, I find. (Cliché? Yes. True? Also yes.) Also, have you noticed – I'm sure you have, that each reverberation, each returning echo is quieter than the one that went before. Keep making the same mistakes and eventually the price you pay is so small it really doesn't signify.

You've been so quiet for the last half hour, which is strange and beyond generously kind. Thank you so much for listening while I wang on about a nearly-affair. No, it was stupid, really. Nothing in the grand scheme of things. It was over many years ago and truthfully long before it began, if that makes sense. It changed me, but it didn't touch me.

Your eyes are sparkling, magnetic, tell me you're amused by my folly, yes? I know, I was a lot younger then – more vulnerable.

Oh god, me boring on has wasted some of our precious time together. I'm so sorry, I'm really here because I want to learn more about you. Would it be terribly forward if we held hands across the table while you told me your story? I really want to learn everything there is to know about you.

No, Marek is long, long gone – it was a decade ago, more.

But from the moment I first heard your story I felt a connection. Thank you for being vulnerable, for sharing with me. Your writing about your experiences, honestly, it floored me. You held a mirror up to reality and found it lacking.

Your palm is so soft against my lips, oh, I hadn't expected your skin to smell of cinnamon and, is it, coconut? But then also salt, and the sea. Your thoughts, as expressed in your writing – Christ, reading you, it's like diving into an ocean.

No, I mean, yes, I had imagined what your skin might smell of because you've filled my thoughts and imaginings since that first DM, before. I'd – God, I sound like a stalker – been following you, reading you, for months before I got up the courage to reach out.

Yeah, exactly. That's it, as I said. I like the way you write, which means I like the way you think.

Lisa Westhaven

Last week's roses

The roses you gave me last week are dead
Their petals have fallen away.
They wait like frail old ladies
With tissues and talcum in tinder hands
Loose wedding bands on kindling fingers
By the garbage bin . . .
Last week's roses

Crushed upon egg shells and rinds of bacon.
Dusky-pink ladies wait
Soaking in tea leaf messages
Blurred honey-sweet words on a sodden card.
The roses, the ladies, the loving thoughts
Once rigid and rife with budding life.
Now fetid and fertile with death.

Judith Dowling

One of life's greatest gifts

Life will hit you where it hurts the most.
There are times you will sink so low you'll never feel like
getting up again. Like you've been imprisoned in the
cold entrapment of an endless abyss with no way out.
It's in these moments, when the world itself turns its
back on you, when every day feels like just another step
toward the grave and the grave seems like the only
place you'll ever get to be at peace,
These moments when you feel like you have nothing
else that you must preserve the one solitary element
that will get you through experiences that a bulletproof
vest couldn't-
You have to preserve hope. Only without it are you truly
lost

One of life's greatest gifts is the sudden rays of light-
These unforeseen breaks in the shadows that have
enveloped us
And these radiant luminations are shining in... from
your past

Your own doings are only historical once you are.
The people you meet, the talents you learn and
accomplishments you make are treasure chests that are
bound to reopen

Know that a miracle happens when it is least expected
and most needed

So hold on to hope, let it be your best friend.
It will be there for you, even if nobody else is.

And in those destructive times, when you've earned a
miracle,
That miracle could save your life

Maxim Anderson

Generations

Each day
Grandfather and granddaughter
walk into the sunlight,
aiming for the park

once brave and strong as a Toledo bull
he now slowly shuffles in his past
terrified of his own transience

.

holding tightly his calloused hand,
she baby skips into her free future,
terrified of nothing

bound by love, blood, need,
so much depends upon
each of them
remembering

Sandra Lanteri

Wycheproof

The steam train puffed into the Wycheproof Station. Oll, her fair curly headed baby in her arms, stepped onto the platform followed by Bob, Rob and Lauren. The hush. The warm, gentle breeze. The vast blue sky. Eucalypts whispering. In the distance, flatness, while in the foreground, field upon field of golden wheat.

Rob and Lauren ran down the platform in sheer jubilation, gazed at the corrugated iron toilet, then ran back to their parents.

WYCHEPROOF

Lauren spelt it out loud. "What a funny name? What does it mean, Dad?"

"It's an aboriginal name *Witchi-poorf Witchie* means the plant and *poorf* is the top of the hill, so Wycheproof means the plants or trees growing on the top of the hill," he said.

"Is that where the word 'witchety grub' comes from?" Lauren asked.

'Could be," Bob said.

"Where's the hill?" Rob wanted to know.

"Over there." Bob pointed to the east. "They call it Mount Wycheproof.'

"What are they, Dad?" Rob asked, pointing to the other side of the railway line.

"Wheat silos," he said, fast running out of patience.

The stationmaster's office, fresh from a coat of bold paint, shimmered in the heat.

"Let's make ourselves known," Bob said.

The porter, on duty that day, stepped forward when he saw the family.

"Welcome," he said. He shook Bob by the hand. His face was as tan as Bob's brown, leather shoes.

The familiar scene in the office - brown wooden counter, iron scales, pigeon holes, typewriter, morse code beeper and the clock with the Roman numerals.

"Come on," Bob said. "Let's find our house."

They walked down Railway Parade toward the Calder Highway.

"Will we be living there?" Rob asked when he saw the row of railway houses.

"No, we'll be living near the mount."

They turned into the highway and came to a dam.

"That's where the water is stored to make steam for the train engines. It comes from a pipe further up the mount," Bob said.

"A railway line down the middle of the main street!" Whatever would they see next?

"It goes all the way to Mildura," Bob said.

"SEA LAKE?" Lauren had caught sight of yet another sign. "Is there really a sea?"

"There was once, long, long ago, before you were born. But it's dead and buried now," Bob said.

A row of peppercorn trees, trunks gnarled with age. Rose pink peppercorns.

"Goody, goody," Rob said. "I'll use them for my pea shooter."

They passed Centenary Park, the Terminus Hotel, Homelhoff's Butchers and turned into Mount Street. A dog with a brown smudge on its face trotted up to Bob. "Woof," it said. "Woof. Woof." Bob patted its nose. It ran off, satisfied.

Ripples of clay coloured sand, the soft north wind playing a warm, elemental welcome to the strangers. They hoped the townsfolk would receive them with a similar embrace.

"There's Mount Wycheproof," Rob cried when the mount came into view. "Can we go there and play?"

"No," Oll said. "Definitely not." She was looking for the address Bob had been given by the porter.

"This must be it," Bob said. His jaw dropped. Another dump, in little better shape than the previous one. "I'll soon find something better; you wait and see."

~ ~ ~

Oll, dressed in a light summer frock, put Alan in the pusher and, with Rob on one side and Lauren on the other, they visited the mount.

"That's not a mount!" Rob said as they drew near. While it looked like a hill (it rose one hundred and forty feet above the plains), it had the distinction of being the lowest registered mount in the world. To Lauren, it was more than a mount, it was magic. She imagined the aborigines camped beneath the black wattles, the wallabies leaping across the sparsely treed plain at the foot of the mount and an emu sauntering with its brood. She took a leaf from a mallee gum, broke it in two and breathed in the aromatic perfume.

They climbed to the summit and gazed over the flat sandy earth. Oll pointed out the reservoir for the town's water supply and the grain silos that held wheat and barley. That day she was radiant. Her sparkling grey eyes danced with fun and laughter. While she kept a watch over Alan, Rob and Lauren explored the mount. Afterwards, they lay spread eagled on the sand, their young bodies absorbing the warm earth beneath. A little later, their mother's voice sounded through the stillness.

"Time to go."

The two older children were thoughtful as they made their way home and were pleased when their mother promised to take them to the mount another time.

'Why can't we go on our own?" Rob asked.

"Because it's unsafe."

"Why?"

Oll kept her thoughts to herself. One time, she'd been told, a child had climbed the water tower, had fallen in and drowned. She didn't want anything to happen to her children.

Lorraine Doney

Dreams of a life

I saw her by the window, old Mrs whatshername
Her frail tissue paper hands parting the yellowed
curtains
As she peered out
To see if life still went on without her

Her world now confined to the bed, the kitchen, the
bathroom,
perhaps a precious moment taking sun on the porch
maybe a visit to the doc.
"The time's approaching;
you'll need to think about care"
Words spoken to so many of her age

I shuddered to think to become so old and hurried on.

But old Mrs whatshername,
Was somewhere off in her dreaming past
Hair caught in a jaunty pony tail, flared taffeta pink skirt,
A naughty hint of lipstick
and oh those sneakers, just made for dancing
As her handsome Bob moved her to the beat
twirling her, whirling her
Her heart racing with the giddy joy
of all that life might bring
"You're my best girl Pat — I love ya"

And their life together had been just so
Full of love and squabbles, children loved and mourned,
dancing, travels, health and illness
and so much more.

I saw her sitting on her porch
The setting sun highlighting creased cheeks
I ventured up the path, offered a smile, an introduction.
She offered a seat.

"So Pat, tell me all about your life – I bet you've got
some stories there."

Sharon Hurst

Self worth status

She craved your approval
Your precious approval
Like a jewel
It was rare for you to give it away
She only craved it more
For if she worked hard enough
Maybe one day she'd have enough to make a necklace
She'd wear it every day
To show the world she was worthy of love
Only to notice the most beautiful people didn't wear
any jewellery at all

Jess Walters

Journey to belonging

7.45am. At our local station we wait for the train. Notice us. Young, singular, polished, contained. A certain brittleness links us in our determination to be at the cutting edge of the good life.

We wait nonchalantly, eyeing each other's trendy gear, echoed on the billboards around us; acknowledging our matching body language, and understanding our niche of belonging. *Get head hunted while craving our morning coffee,* the billboards promise, and *Win a trip to L.A. every day, where high rises blot out the sky.*

We wait with a certain smugness. Pretty boys in uniform black. Shark-eyed real estate dudes, in shiny shoes. Smooth middle managers, sans tie, and me, one of the treacle-haired advertising executives in designer shades, sipping skinny soy lattes from designer cups. Food for the day.

I am them. They are me. I belong here. Then last week, a letter from a stranger arrived. A woman who wants to meet me. If I meet her, everything familiar to me could change. I could lose the order and the security of my place here. What then will I become? Where then will I belong? To get on this train is to gamble, and the stakes are high. After a sleepless night, I have decided to take the risk.

So, now I'm on this speeding train, and the longest day of my life stretches before me. I'm going to Sydney to meet the stranger, the woman who gave me away. The mother I have never known. For years I have dismissed her for abandoning me. I have never looked for her. I didn't want to be rejected twice, then her letter arrived. Why has she waited so long to contact me? Is she dying? Why did she abandon me, I have asked myself over the years. I have tried to put her out of my mind, but she keeps returning.

Outside this train, the countryside rushes by. I see a trio of black swans gliding on a still lake. Across a paddock, horses wearing green coats, are standing together talking over the day. Further on, serried ranks of open-mouthed freight cars lie rotting in a Jeffrey Smart landscape, near new-born lambs, and just past Goulburn station, darklystraight poplars remind me of distant Tuscany. By observing in detail my surroundings, I'm hoping to still my mind. It's my fragile ploy to get me through the day.

Inside this carriage, an incessant army of people on the move, swaying unsteadily along the too narrow aisles. Probably off to buy a pie, chips, a coke, a beer, or a nice cup of tea. Eating, I suppose, is one way to while away the hours. Maybe she was young and had no choice but to give me up. I suppose it would have been hard in those days to keep me. Society thinking has changed now. It's so much easier for girls to keep their babies. I have.

Inside this train, the easy *bonhomie* of the trapped ordinary is extraordinary. I see the way complete strangers easily exchange their stories. I have never done that. Could never do that. What will my mother disclose? My father's name perhaps?

As the day progresses, unravelling happens. Coats are discarded, newspapers scatter,

mobiles ring nonstop, and kids fight over games. Do I have siblings? I watch an old couple sleeping, hand in hand, while coke cans roll willy-nilly, up and down the aisle, a symphony of tinny sounds around their deaf ears. Do I have grandparents?

So many questions. As the day grows long sharp edges blur, and I am nervous. Will I like her? Will she like me?

In the late afternoon sun, the unique Australian countryside I have always loved rushes by, echoing Fred William's hills, and Streeton's wonderful jacaranda blue. Did I get my love of art from her? Could she be a country girl? Perhaps she's feeling like me right now. How will I know her? What will I say? Are there the words?

Shadows lengthen as arrival approaches. Last minute conversations are had, and I see some people exchange mobile numbers. How nice to see friendships have been made. Coats are put on, and people drag heavy suitcases from the overhead racks. And I am here, with my inner drama and racing heart, so apart from the flurry of all this movement. Take away my fears. Take away my anger, my hurt. Take away my years of questioning. Very soon now I will meet the mother who gave me life.

As the rhythm of the metal boxes slows, there is a quiet clapping as the train glides into another successful completion. Sydney is out the door. Is this my new beginning, a new belonging, or another leaving?

With my heart pounding, I search the platform looking for the mother I have never known. And then I see her. I recognise her at once. She looks just like me. Just like me. See us Universe, Mother and daughter. An easy intimacy, a belonging has already begun, and we are smiling as we walk towards each other.

Sandra Lanteri

Crones

We are the crones, still alive, still kicking
against the pricks who manifest in many
guises but gain no ground with us, ever.

If we are withered, let us find in fallen jowls
and rippling wrinkles, the wisdom of our lives
cast on rocks from which we've scrambled,

not to safety, but to all our dangerous pursuits —
like giving birth and climbing mountains, day
after day, committing continuous acts of courage.

Wisdom is the word that defines our destiny;
our withered flowers fall to enrich the earth
in anonymity, lightly, fearlessly growing another

generation of girls and boys in waves of strength
to weave their way into a brave new world,
spun in intricate patterns of upbringing.

If we are fearsome, so let it be for those who fear
hook-nosed telling of the truth, out of our long
past, our shorter future, we rhyme the remains.

Ann Simic

Mao's Great Mango Parade: 1968

In 1968, our compound's Uncle Wang had the grand title of Revolutionary Messenger for the Telecommunications Post Office compound, Baotou, Inner Mongolia – which actually meant that he had to call out messages for the revolutionary meetings with his loud-as-a-thunder-clap voice every year between 1966 and 1976.

Uncle Wang seemed like an ancient man. I knew two types of old people – those who were old, and those who were near death. If they still smiled from time to time, they were old. If they did not smile any more, they were near death. Uncle Wang certainly was the latter. Years later, I would find out that he wasn't as old as I thought – he just looked that way.

He had droopy, puffy eyes like a basset hound. He was nearly as tall as my grandpa, who was 188 centimetres tall. His back was slightly stooped, but he walked with giant steps.

Uncle Wang's actual job was to deliver the personal messages for the Compound, because we did not have telephones in our houses. The entire Compound only had one telephone – a black thing that lived in his room.

Three generations of Compound residents had addressed him as Uncle Wang, even though he was related to none of us. He was very well respected for doing an excellent job of delivering the messages with his gigantic voice.

On the evening of Monday, 5 August 1968, Uncle Wang

made a significant announcement.

"Revolutionary comrades!" he boomed. "There is going to be a piece of important news on the Central People's Broadcasting Station – China's National Radio! Please come to the loudspeaker pole to listen to the eight o'clock news tonight!"

It was a warm later-summer evening, the gentle Inner Mongolian breeze blowing on our faces as we all crowded near the loudspeaker pole in the oval in the centre of the compound. The sun still shone brilliantly. All 180 families who lived in our compound were there. Every adult worked for the same company that Uncle Wang did – the combined Telecommunications and Post Office company. Very few people could afford a radio, so the loudspeaker had been installed in the middle of the oval.

We stood around the pole with anticipation. Lingling and I, along with all our other friends, were running through and sometimes under the adults' legs. After the static sound of a clock beeping the hour echoed across the oval, the anticipated announcement began.

"The last beep was Beijing Time: eight o'clock," the reporter announced before the signature music reached our ears. Everyone stood erect and quiet. The male Xinhua newsreader read the report in a dignified voice.

"The president of Congo gave our great leader Mao Zedong two *mang guos*. His Elderly sent the two *mang guos* to the workers out of love for the working class. This noble deed is worthy of celebration. Mao Zedong, His Elderly, is a truly great leader."

We all referred to honoured old people as 'His Elderly' or 'Her Elderly'. It was a mark of great respect. 'His Elderly', as a term, had attached to Mao Zedong, especially during the Cultural Revolution.

Aunty Li, one of the three well-known active revolutionary participants from the telecommunications company, spoke loudly to the crowd, which was excited to boiling point at tis moment. "It is truly exciting news! His Elderly's generosity is worthy of a celebration!" Everyone cheered and clapped at the mention of our great leader and his generosity. Eyes welled with tears, reflecting the golden glow of the light on top of the pole; hearts swelled with gratitude at his generosity. We were ecstatic – even though none of us had even the faintest idea what *mang guos* were, although the character *guo* suggested some kind of fruit.

"Revolutionary comrades," Uncle Wang's voice echoed behind the crowd again, "The leader of the company has asked you all to go to the hall and make a model *mang guo* for tomorrow's parade. Please participate with enthusiasm."

Everyone in the compound marched to the hall in high spirits. To my disappointment, my mother told my brother and me to go home. We would have to be up early in the morning to join the *mang guo* parade, and we needed our sleep. Grandma was visiting us at the time. She looked after us during the time our parents took part in activities such as this.

The following day was a cheerful August morning with hazy orange sunshine. Teacher Chen from the school said to my class, "Our great leader, Chairman Mao, is such a selfless person; he did not eat the two *mang guos* himself, and instead he gave them to the workers. His action really touches our hearts. We ought to be loyal to His Elderly for the rest of our lives.'

Silently, we all listened and felt excited. After Teacher Chen spoke, Headmaster Zhang addressed the whole school assembly with his village accent.

"Chairman Mao is our thoughtful leader, and he is very busy with his work for the whole country, and yet he gets in touch with common people such as workers in the factories. We need to carry out His Elderly's Revolution for the rest of our lives." Headmaster Zhang had begun life as a poor peasant and had achieved his high position as headmaster courtesy of Chairman Mao's policies.

The weather was warm and the air smelt fresh as we marched on the broad asphalt road with dirt path on the side. Shops lined our journey up the main street of Baotou.

A truck cruising slowly in the front led the parade. On top of it, there was a gigantic oval-shaped object as wide as the truck. It was made out of wires with paper glued over the outside of it. The strange object had an orange tinge in the middle, making the effect a smooth orange ball.

The truck was followed by hundreds of workers from the Baotou Steelworks, both men and women wearing their identical uniforms of blue denim jackets, trousers and denim caps on their heads. The working suits replaced Mao's green suits for a while on the streets. They had a tool-belt each dangling on their bottoms, with pliers, a spanner and different-sized screwdrivers with colourful handles. They looked heavy to carry around, but the workers carried them with dignity.

My school was well known for having a good headmaster and being the most active school in carrying out the revolution in Baotou. In light of this, we were the first school to follow the workers and we followed them with pride. The students made up a big part of the parade. We all strutted proudly with our red armbands around our left arms. Lingling and I were holding a red banner with the words: *"Long live the Mao Zedong's thoughts."*

Students carried big drums on their fronts and had gongs

strapped to their hands. One short boy, our class captain, was leading us shouting slogans: "Long live Chairman Mao! Long live the Cultural Revolution! Annihilate the enemies!" Sometimes, the class captain failed to select the appropriate slogan for the occasion.

We wore solemn faces as we chanted along with him. Our backs were straight and proud; our steps were brisk in time with the drumbeats, full of revolutionary vigour. And we sang our favourite song: *Sailing the sea depends on the helmsman* – which was a special song devoted to Mao Zedong.

> *'Sailing the seas depends on the helmsman.*
> *Life and growth depend on the sun.*
> *Rain and dewdrops nourish the crops.*
> *Making revolution depends on Mao Zedong's Thought.*
> *Fish can't leave the water.*
> *Nor melons leave the vine.*
> *The revolutionary masses can't do without the communist party.*
> *Mao Zedong's thought is the sun that shines forever.'*

We all wore our special uniforms, white blouses or shirts, navy blue trousers, and black corduroy shoes. We walked four students abreast, many rows of students, walking with importance past the spectators – mainly elderly women – who stood on the dirt paths smiling admiringly at us. I smiled cheerfully back at them. Suddenly, I saw my grandma and her friend, whom we called Su's Mother-in-law. She was from another village from Inner Mongolia. She was quite a humorous old lady; Grandma loved to laugh at her jokes. Grandma and Su's Mother-in-law became quite good friends while they visited their daughters, and they had picked up another old lady along the way to form an elderly gang of three.

Grandma came over to me while we were marching on

the spot at the city centre for inspection. "What is a *mang guo?*" she asked.

"Shhhhh, lower your voice, Grandma," I said quietly. I was embarrassed that she did not know what a *mang guo* was (even though I didn't know either). "I think it is a fruit, from the character *guo*, but I don't know what *mang* means," I whispered in a low voice.

Her new friend stepped forward to us, and said in her southern accent, "It is a fruit, as big as a fist. It is very sour."

"From the model on the truck, it is a mighty big fruit. How big do you think the tree would be?" Su's Mother-in-law had a sarcastic tone in her voice.

A woman in worker's uniform, who had overheard their disrespectful chatter, looked over with big wide-open eyes.

"Be quiet, you old women!' she growled. 'You are all counterrevolutionaries. Someone should report you to the state. You don't want to insult Chairman Mao's fruit, do you?"

The three old ladies moved back to the crowd on the dirt path. They dared not retort, because the woman could indeed have reported them and they could have been in a lot of trouble. The government didn't like people who disrespected the Chairman in any way, or his fruit.

We all admired the uniforms of the workers as we marched by. After all Chairman Mao gave the fruit to them, the workers.

"They look good, don't you think?' said a student girl in my line, pointing at the workers. We all knew that the workers in uniforms were the most trusted by the Chairman. For now.

While I liked their uniforms, I did not envy their tool-belts. I thought they did not look scholarly. I only admired people who looked more educated. I believed grandma's aspiration that I was going to university – being a worker did not appeal to me. Still, I could not tell anyone about my plan; being intellectual meant being beaten up physically and being branded as 'smelly'. Naturally, children did not look up to intellectuals. Not publically anyway.

"Have you ever heard of such a fruit?" I asked the girl who had pointed to the workers' uniforms. I knew her mother was not only a policewoman but also she was in charge of the local police station – a very high-ranking woman indeed. This girl's family might have seen a lot more than Lingling and me.

"No," she replied, "though my mother might know. I'll ask her." She was always proud of her mother. Then she moved forward, and said to one of the older women in workers uniform, "Aunty, do you know what a *Mang guo* is?"

The woman looked us with a look of concern and said, "I don't know anything! Don't ask silly questions! You could get me into trouble by asking me.' She looked around her fearfully to see if anyone had heard her. We looked at each other guiltily. We all knew politics was not something we should talk about – but sometimes in the excitement, we forgot. We also knew the fear of being reported. We all knew people who had been reported – and if children were reported, their parents were punished.

Being talkative had caused lots of trouble for ordinary people during the Cultural Revolution. My uncle Zhao, my father's friend, was purged as a rightist. The only thing he said was the tiny windows in the newly built houses looked like the windows of jails. For this comment, he had been singled out and jailed.

Behind my pride and smile, I gazed upon the giant model

mang guo on the truck bathed in the golden ray of sunshine. It was glowing with light, the shiny paper reflecting the sun. It was smooth where the paper joined; it must have taken them a long time to make it.

In my nine-year-old thinking, if this was a fruit, why would we parade with it? Were adults always right in their decision-making, I wondered. Well, perhaps some adults were correct, they said if our Chairman said so, it must be right. I guessed, no one dared to question it, or your enemies would wage it as a weapon to attack you. After all, Mother snatching that little bag of power was genuine because Chairman Mao had encouraged them to do it. I'd better not to think too much about it. Who knew what trouble I could course by overthinking?

After the parade, the telecommunications company for whom my parents worked positioned their model *mang guo* on a platform in their building's main hall. It would remain there for months. Before each meeting, people went up to the model *mang guos* with Chairman Mao's portrait above on the wall, to bow to Mao's portrait and the model *mang guos*. They silently asked Mao for revolutionary instructions in the morning and reported their revolutionary success in the evening.

Later I heard some bits and pieces from different people about the two *mang guos* that were given to Mao Zedong and which he handed down to the workers. A *mang guo* was a subtropical fruit and was very nutritious. It was hailed as the king of tropical fruit. In northern China, we did not grow this kind of fruit because of the cold climate.

I gave some more thought to it, and the idea entered my head that when Mao gave the fruit to the workers he, just maybe, did not like the fruit. My father did not like fruit much and never ate any apples. In fact, people in my

Grandma's village said that apples were like 'horse-fart bubbles'. My neighbour told me that in Inner Mongolia, we did not grow apples. The apples we had were imported from the southern part of China. By the time the apples reached Inner Mongolia, they had lost their crunchiness. The softness of the apple gave them the derogatory name.

Just as I would leave the Cultural Revolution, I would leave this episode behind me, never had learned what a *mang guo* was. Until one day, many decades later, I would be given a mango, in Australia. All of a sudden, it was like a window flashed open in front of me, and I realised the *mang guo* we were parading with was actually the same as the mango I was then eating.

Later I read about this incident from various sources and it was true that Mao did not like the fruit at all. Therefore he gave the mangoes to the workers. Why workers? Mao was a talented political craftsman. At the beginning of the Cultural Revolution, he instigated the campaign of Red Guards destroying the Four Olds – Old Customs, Old Culture, Old Habits and Old Ideas. Red Guards mostly consisted of teenage students and they did a very good job of smashing the Old Fours. Somehow they did too good a job, and it was reported back to Mao that the Red Guards were out of hand. He was very concerned and so utilised the strategy of sending the Red Guards to the countryside to receive re-education from the peasants. He began to promote the workers and, as a result, 'Work Teams' were organised and were sent to every company to push people in 'moving the revolution' forward.

Mao Zedong's personal physician Li Zhisui later wrote in his book that the same factory workers held a ceremony to welcome the mangoes and that this involved singing Mao Zedong's quotations. They even waxed the two mangoes and placed them on a table in their hall intending to preserve the mangoes for their offspring. After the two mangoes had gone rotten inside the wax, they made real images out of wax so that they could still bow to the mangoes. It did not make any difference to them that the mangoes were dead inside.

When Li Zhisui told this story to Mao Zedong in his memoir, he laughed, and said, 'it does not hurt anyone if they blindly admire mangoes.' He was quite right about it. From then on, almost every family had waxed mangoes on their dinner tables. Many also hung paintings of mangoes. Mangoes became the sacred fruit in China.

The mango parade was one glimpse of The Great Proletarian Cultural Revolution of China. It was a remarkable show of how one deft politician could evoke such a mass emotion from ordinary people.

Zhiling Gao

Commuting

smiling over a river is the closest I'll get to sonder
in this frightfully singular
abstractly contagious hell
I wonder if the grubby silme I slick on my cheeks in the
night actually boils the dirt stuck in my chin
or vaporises it
might be better if it would
vaporise that scratching sound
it's the cricket itching its legs
it's the fish breathing through water (barely)
it's the thrumming of crawfish clawfish
hello! he cries! I made noise! I make noise!
they do not apologise, the creatures in the river
I walk by them,
we mention each other in passing on Tuesdays.
the tight nod shows we are made of each other but,
honestly, not really friends.

Lucy Tomov

Woman

Far into the heart of Uluru's ancient shadow
close by the stillness of the sacred Mutitjulu waterhole
right where the full moon dances its sad sorry song
and the spirit of the gum trees
nourishes the deep red earth
the woman
lies down
 in the womb of the circle
she has traced in the sand

Into it she gathers her ancestor-heroes
her sweet wild lovers
her lost stolen children
her bondage years of toil

then
ancient rufous hare-wallaby watching
baby locks shielding blind eyes
from the glare
 of too much truth
 she begins the delicate business of
becoming

Sandra Lanteri

Total information awareness

Chapter 1

"Is this something you're used to doing?" she asked.

"Pouring my own wine?" the accented woman responded. The service here was terrible but only because they were strangely accommodating a small wedding- let's assume because of the virus. A distressed waiter made eye contact across the room with her but she smiled and dismissively shook her head to indicate she had it under control and not to worry.

"I meant blind dates. This is new to me. My goodness, I've only had school dates or dates from work. Ha! So, tell me about your work?" The confidence of the wine gave her a lingering stare she would otherwise be uncomfortable giving.

"I sell things to people who don't need them. It takes up time and has me travelling a lot. I'm really looking to get out, to tell you the truth." She stared down at her glass which she had overfilled. "Unnecessary stress. I don't like my employer, and I'd like to retire."

"Maybe your new life is with me? Ha! The wine is talking. Where is our food?"

The wedding bustles.

Chapter 2

"This is the most recent photo of Anatoly Khodorkovsky's wife alive?" the senior Russian bureaucrat asked.

"Yes, from seven years ago. Our artificial intelligence found it while scanning social media. It's from a wedding video."

He played the video and froze it in one of the few frames that captured her perfectly clearly. The cameraman's attention had been elsewhere.

"Log it. Inform the minister."

Nathan Clark

Scanning

The crowded crowd at the concert tells me again and
again I am in the way
I become a boulder blocking the boulevard to
his friend,
their prime position,
and her toilet break
When you leave, your place is replaced by shuffling feet
and foreign body heat
When you return I realise I am no longer in the way
I am the way

Jess Walters

Monsoon

Storms crash in on masses of dark clouds, waterfalls
pour from the sky and scatter; perched on a porch,
slouched in steamy heat, I turn to the tortured purple
sky, catch the flicker of lightning, the grumble of
thunder, the wailing wind, the startled twist and toss of
coconut trees.

Bang! The deluge hammers and scars tin roofs,
bounces, batters, darts, in thunderstruck sheets, lashes
overflowing eaves, slaps, strikes full force, wary, wired,
spooked by a screaming sea of sound.

Temperatures plummet, shivering air stomps in,
enraged, breathless; trees washed green, denuded,
toppled, a glistening, polished, chaotic world
unearthed.

On a beach somewhere in Southern India, the monsoon
crashes in, decked in full regalia. I observe all alone,
wide-eyed, wild-eyed, from my protected place; rain
rattles windows, gutters gurgle, frogs hide.

A sudden urge to rush outside, collide with a headlong
tide, dive drenched heater-skelter for cover.
The torrent carpet-bombs devastated land.
I slip, swash and spatter, stagger towards safety.

Emerald green leaves slap me
bejewelled, torn petals slump,
spider webs sag.

Quick as it comes, it goes, the sticky rain; Indra, keeper
of the skies, of lightning, thunder, clouds, has spoken.
The ground around steams with wiggling geckos,
darting frogs, snaking anaconda.

The drama is done. Vehicles in the wake of lashing rain,
still ground to a halt, rivers where pavements were,
and, in the hotel lobby, a lake.

Time for a cold beer, to sit and marvel at the aftermath
until all dissolves into silence, until steamy humidity
embraces everyone who ventures out into this bright,
scented, luminous world, forgetting the next cataclysm.

Ann Simic

Cradling Daddy

Breakfast on the Danube's Gellert Hotel terrace. "Yu are ze Flower-ov Love"! In a crunchy Polish accent, a passing young lady mouthed gently at seeing me feed the doves. They were peck-pecking at the seeds like mad. Her melting looks implied she would have done so herself, despite the "tsk, tsk" frowns of some of the other breakfast gobbling la-di-dah posh guests.

She stopped by. I asked, "Do you know why these toffs are angry at the doves?"

"They need love," she said.

I sat stunned.

She didn't mean the doves.

A touch to my shoulder, and she went, compliantly following her husband, a man vaguely annoyed.

On the train ride to *Szobathely*. I saw one hundred blackbirds stand statue in a field. Also, three big deers equally motionless on the forest's edge. Through the three rattling hours of land, I didn't see one single *marha*, which in Hungarian means 'idiot, but in English are called even more detestably 'stock'. In Hungarian the word *marha* means 'idiot'. You wonder, does a slur like that make it easier to bomp them on the head with a club to crack their skulls? As for goats, sheep, pigs, lambs, - where are they! I saw none. They have been locked up. Usually for life. Robbed of even one minute in nature, of life in a paddock, grazing under trees, or just to stand on happy grass, or living under the sky! They were all squashed into barns cages, pens, or strapped for the entirety of their wretched existence onto metal sties.

At the Szombathely's Wagner Hotel. The vision of this morning's garden is of its red furred athlete, an auburn squirrel looping from tree to tree. The feeling is, of having everything. Acrobatics! Beauty! Spring! Except, locked in one of the rooms, there's the starting up yelps of a dog, his howls of fear and craving shoots into the hotel garden's green silence. But breakfast ends. The dog's weep stops. And on his personal hotel-terrace sits the owner. And with paws paddling the air, tongue lolling on the lap of his now kissy-cuddly, cradling daddy, his love justified – the perky and funny, the smiley retriever.

Katherine Hoffman

Time

Time, this unseen element that exists everywhere
Make you win, make you lose and it doesn't care

You keep running to destroy its arrogance, yet it defeats
you with no hesitation
So you ask for a peace agreement, you ask for a
conciliation

It is a wild horse in need of taming.
So take responsibility with no blaming

It is your treasure, don't waste it for silly things
It is your fortune, make it worth it in everything.

Rahaf Al Maalouf

The first date

Lawrence sat at his desk, staring at his computer screen. It had been six months since his wife had passed away, and he was lonely. He had never been very good at meeting women, and now that he was in his mid-forties, he felt like his chances were dwindling.

Lawrence had heard of online dating, but it had always seemed a bit desperate to him. Still, he couldn't deny the appeal of being able to connect with someone from the comfort of his own home. He had created a profile on a dating site and had been browsing through potential matches for the past hour.

Lawrence stared glassy-eyed at his computer screen. He had been scrolling through dating websites for hours, but nothing seemed to catch his interest. He was tired of meaningless flings and casual hook-ups. What he really wanted was a connection with someone. Someone who understood him, who shared his interests, and who could be there for him through thick and thin.

Just as he was about to log off, a profile caught his eye. Her name was Maryam, and she was a doctor. She was also Muslim, which intrigued him. He had never dated anyone outside of his own faith before, but he had always been open to the idea. He was a Jewish lawyer, also living in Australia. They were both in their mid-40s, and both had experienced the pains of loss and loneliness. The only commonalities that Lawrence could find were a love for music and singing, and the fact that they were both desperate to make a connection. They were both lonely.

And so the contact began. He sent her a message, and to his surprise, she responded quickly. They began chatting online, and he found himself looking forward to their conversations. They talked about everything from their jobs to their favourite books, and he felt a sense of connection with her that he had never felt with anyone else.

As the weeks went by, their conversations became more personal. He learned that she had never been married and had always been focused on her career. She, in turn, learned about his late wife and the pain he had gone through after losing her.

Their conversations were the highlight of his day, and he found himself wishing he could meet her in person. But he knew that it would be complicated. They were from vastly different backgrounds, and he wasn't sure how they would navigate the cultural differences. But something about Maryam's messages had intrigued him, and he found himself looking forward to her responses.

They exchanged photos, and Lawrence was struck by how beautiful Maryam was. There was something about her warm, brown eyes and gentle smile that drew him in.

As they continued to talk, Lawrence began to realize that he was falling for Maryam. He had never felt such a strong connection with anyone before. He found himself thinking about her all the time.

One day, Maryam surprised him with her suggestion.

"Hey Lawrence, are you still interested in meeting up? I know we come from different worlds, but I think we have a lot in common. Let's meet up at Cafe Timbuktu in Brighton this Saturday. It's in Wilson Street. I'll be there at

6 pm. Hope to see you."

Lawrence hesitated for a moment before typing out a response. "I'll be there. Looking forward to it."

He closed his laptop and leaned back in his chair, feeling a mix of nervousness and excitement. He had never been on a date with someone he had met online, and he wasn't sure what to expect. But he was intrigued by Maryam, and was keen to see if the connection they had in the virtual world was mirrored in the real world. He wanted to see her, to touch her, to hear her sing. He knew it was risky, but he'd already decided it was worth taking the chance.

***

Lawrence sat in his car outside Cafe Timbuktu, feeling a mix of anticipation and dread. He had spent the past hour trying to decide what to wear, and he had settled on a pair of dark jeans and a button-up shirt. He had even splashed on a bit of cologne, hoping to make a good impression.

He stepped out of the car and walked towards the restaurant. He saw Maryam sitting at a table near the window, and his heart skipped a beat. She was even more beautiful than he had imagined, with striking features. He walked over to her table and smiled despite his nervousness.

Maryam was scrolling through her phone, when she saw Lawrence walk in. He was tall and wiry, with a kind face and the same coloured eyes as her own. She stood up to greet him, also feeling the butterflies in her stomach. He was a Jewish man, and she was a Muslim woman. They came from different backgrounds and had different beliefs. She wasn't sure how they could ever find common ground.

"Hi Lawrence. It's good to finally meet you in person," she said, extending her hand.

Lawrence smiled at her. "It's good to meet you too, Maryam. You look even more beautiful in person."

Maryam felt a blush rise to her cheeks. "Thank you."

They sat down across from each other, and Lawrence ordered a coffee.

The dreadful nervousness in the pit of his gut refused to abate. He had been on countless first dates before, but this one felt different. He wanted it to work so badly that it was almost painful.

Maryam looked at him curiously. "You seem nervous," she said.

Lawrence laughed nervously. "I guess I am. This is the first date I've been on in a while."

Maryam nodded in understanding. "Me too. I've never really had time for dating. I've always been focused on my career."

Lawrence smiled at her. "What kind of doctor are you?"

"I'm a paediatrician," Maryam said proudly.

Lawrence raised his eyebrows in surprise. "Wow, that's really impressive. I'm just a lawyer."

Maryam smiled at him. "Don't sell yourself short. Being a lawyer is a noble profession."

Lawrence felt a sense of relief wash over him. Maybe they had more in common than he had initially thought. They spent the next few minutes chatting about their jobs, and Lawrence was struck by how easy it was to talk to her.

As they chatted, Maryam found herself feeling more and more at ease with Lawrence. He was kind and funny, with a quick wit that made her laugh. They shared stories about their childhoods and their families, and Maryam found herself opening up to him in a way she hadn't with anyone else.

They ordered their food, and the conversation turned to their backgrounds. Despite both of them having come from religious families, it appeared they had both decided religious observance was not really their style.

"I tend to view religions as somewhat of a cult," confessed Maryam with a girlish giggle.

"Totally!" exclaimed Lawrence, breathing an inward sigh of relief.

Lawrence didn't want to dominate the conversation, but decided to take the plunge and open up.

"I didn't just dump religion for no good reason. As I got older, I saw it as pointless," Lawrence said, his voice softening. "But the last straw was when I lost my wife to cancer a few years ago,"

Maryam felt a pang of sadness. "I'm sorry for your loss."

Lawrence nodded. "It's been tough, but I've learned to live with it. I think she would have wanted me to be happy."

Maryam felt a sense of admiration for Lawrence's resilience. She had never been married, but she couldn't imagine losing someone she loved so deeply.

Lawrence had mentioned in one of their online chats that he loved to sing, and Maryam had confessed that she did too.

"Do you want to hear me sing something?" Lawrence asked, feeling emboldened.

Maryam smiled. "Of course," she responded, not really imagining he would do it.

Lawrence cleared his throat and began to sing *Can't Help Falling in Love*. His voice was shaky at first, but as he got into the song, his confidence grew. Maryam watched him with a look of rapt attention, and when he finished, she applauded. The party of four at the neighbouring table, intrigued by the romanticism of the moment, clapped enthusiastically.

"That was beautiful, Lawrence. You have a great voice," she said.

Lawrence felt a rush of happiness. He had always been self-conscious about his singing, but Maryam's praise made him feel like maybe he wasn't so bad after all.

Maryam took a deep breath and began to sing a traditional Muslim song in Arabic. Her voice was rich and melodic, and Lawrence was struck by the passion with which she sang. He didn't understand the words, but the emotion in her voice was unmistakable.

"That was amazing, Maryam," he said, his eyes shining with admiration.

They finished their meal and ordered dessert, and the conversation turned to their hopes and dreams. Maryam talked about her love of medicine and her desire to make a difference in the world. Lawrence talked about his work as a lawyer and his passion for social justice.

As they finished their dessert, Maryam felt a sense of sadness. This was the end of their first date, and she didn't want it to be over.

Peter Levy

The Yarra

Sometimes I catch sighs of voices floating through
millennia;
I browse in curves of time among intimations of
immortality,
among day to day lives wafting in on the wind.

Here, where brown metal beams gaze from an industrial
past,
now morphed into an open-space, mezzanine
encounter.
The unfathomable Yarra winds nearby, witness to
change –

it gurgles its never-ending passage to the sea, skirts city
lights.
It comes in peace to Southbank to touch each little life
with history of wide tree-lined streets, period home
hauteur,

Art Deco simplicity, tessellated tile verandahs, stained-glass,
pressed metal, South Wharf, the Charles Grimes Bridge,
mingling now with all that is new – bars and cafes

spilling onto pavements beside the riverfront, boats
plying
the waters observed by shimmering glass apartments
with their pools, spas, steam rooms, gyms – rising to
rooftop lounges that survey the city, seeing cycling and
walking
paths, beaches and markets, all the treasures of the place –
a country town, a community, in the big smoke.

Ann Simic

If only

That song! It seemed to be played so often on the radio these days, on those channels that devoted themselves to a particular decade of nostalgia, to the golden oldies. It was an oldie but a goodie, the sort that wormed its way into your psyche. It spoke to her on some deeply subliminal level, especially the part where the wailing lead guitar sounded like seagulls wheeling and crying over a lonely beach. It always filled her heart with a deep yearning,

The sky was hazy, the waves silver tipped, the chill in the air said winter was not far away. She was doing her daily walk along the beach path on a late autumn afternoon, earphones linked to her playlist entitled "all-time faves". That song was definitely one of her favourites. As the guitar cried its lead break, that old familiar sense of yearning washed over her.

Yearning was one of life's strange emotions – seldom logical, so hard to pin down. Just what was it that she yearned for?

The past? The safe haven of childhood secure in the love of parents? The memory of it was seldom the actuality.

Love? The sort of romantic love that swept you away, made you feel alive, the vision of your beloved filling your every waking hour? Ugh! What a crock! So many of those roller coaster love affairs had been enough to tip her over the edge into depression and self-loathing.

Yearning for excitement in the here and now? Life could be so dull, trudging through the daily routine, trying to create a sense of purpose now that she was retired. Looking at the same face day in, day out over the breakfast table, and having the same petty squabbles over domestrivia and just who should do what in the house. Sure, one could create excitement with a trip, an outing, a get-together, but after those things were done and dusted it was always a return to more of the same.

Feeling herself at risk of lapsing into a state of deep malcontent, she focused back on the song. Here they were, those two lines, the ones she always waited for:

Don't look back you can never look back

Those days are gone forever, I should just let 'em go

It was always those same phrases that sent her off into a reverie of regret. Well, maybe regret was too strong a word, more like a self-indulgent wallow into her past, speculating on what she should have done differently.

If only my parents had given me a piano instead of a guitar. I could have been a good musician.

Despite the disappointment of being denied a piano, the first guitar had nevertheless been pretty exciting at the outset – that five-pound guitar from Brashs in its strangely angular brown cardboard box.. It had steel strings, and, like the lyrics of another song, she played until her fingers literally bled. Her first teacher eventually confessed he had taught her all he knew, and it was time to move on to more serious stuff, so she enrolled with a teacher of classical guitar, practising maybe two hours per day. After the classical lessons she became quite proficient; good enough to play in a concert in the big cathedral at age 15, but she dropped it – just like that, always looking for the next thing to pour her energies into.

If only I hadn't married David when I was so young.

She often wished that when she'd finished university she

had headed out into the big bad world, travelling, working in Europe, immersing in new cultures and languages. And yet she had been lucky to have travelled much in her life, maybe never long enough to stay in one place and get fluent in any one language, but it had been rewarding and fun. Certainly the Italian she had learned in school had led to a long-standing friendship with a pen pal, and though she often wished she had learned French instead she never would have met Maria, got to visit her, and still be writing to this day.

If only I had pursued a different career.

She didn't know at seventeen what she wanted to do, so just took the easy way out and became a teacher. Yeah, get that scholarship money. Who cared anyway, she'd probably just become a mother in a couple of years, as so many young women of her vintage did- Marry young, have a family, and regret all those things they could no longer do.

If she had known back then her passion for digging in the dirt and making things grow, for creating beautiful surroundings with trees and flowers, for nurturing tiny seeds into flourishing blooms, she would no doubt have gone down a totally different path. Run a nursery, be a landscape gardener, running a crew of young spunky blokes in Blundstone boots and dirt-covered jeans.

If only I had stayed with David and had a child, like he wanted.

The eternal dilemma of childless women - would life have been so much more fulfilling with one's genetic legacy firmly in place? How would it have felt to hold a warm sweet-smelling baby and watch it grow into a young human, full of promise and hope for the future?

How would it have felt to love someone else unconditionally, and feel secure that in your dotage they would be there to care for you, as you sat drooling in your nursing home chair?

She shook that thought away with a cynical laugh. No guarantees in that department she mused, thinking of her close friends whose children had both strayed onto the path of addiction, and now caused their parents more anguish than was imaginable.

If only I hadn't made that second time around marriage to Richard, thank God I did meet Richard, if only we could have had a child together, thank God we didn't have a child, if only he were more like me . . .

She pulled herself up short with a rare flash of insight. Richard probably wished she were more like him. All those areas in which they seemed to be incompatible, but who was to say her way was right? And being a mirror image of each other would probably not have made for an ideal union.

The internal machinations, self-recriminations and regrets swirled around her head. Richard often accused her of always seeing the negative in life; a glass half-full sort of person. She always retorted by saying she'd rather be proven right, than have high expectations and be disappointed.

Her aching back reminded her that perhaps she had walked a little too long. Maybe it was time to call it quits and head for home. Oh hell, she'd have to prepare a meal. She wasn't in the mood for it.

If only Richard were more keen on cooking. The few dishes he prepared were invariably laced with so much chili she barely eat them.

With a sigh she settled behind the wheel, turned on the radio and then turned the wheel in the direction of home. By one of those freak coincidences in life, the very song that had set off her train of thought was blaring out of her car speakers, on its last few bars. As it faded out, the announcer prattled on about how good the 80s were, and introduced the next track - a jarring heavy metal rock anthem.

She reached across to press the knob to change the station, glancing down as she did so. In that split second of distraction she didn't notice a white sedan pushing its way onto the main thoroughfare, accelerating madly and cutting across her path. Too late she slammed on the brakes as the car clipped her front fender.

Her heart leapt into her throat as she shakily pulled into the kerb and turned off the ignition. Several choice curses sprang from her lips. She looked ahead expecting to see the culprit pulled up in front of her, so that they could do the mandatory exchange of licenses and insurance details. But there he or she was . . .zooming ahead up the road, disappearing into the distance, far exceeding the speed limit.

Nervously she got out of the car and walked around to the front, fearing the worst and feeling furious at herself, even though the other party was technically in the wrong. There it was, a ragged scrape in the fender, but surprisingly, not as ghastly as she had expected. Her brain started racing again. *If only I hadn't leaned across to change that radio station.* Richard will be furious.

Resuming her place behind the wheel she quickly discovered that the ugly dent had in no way impaired the car's ability to resume its homeward journey. Twenty minutes later she pulled into the driveway. To her surprise Richard was standing there, beaming from ear to ear.

"You know I just had the feeling you'd be arriving now,"

he said, leaning across to plant a kiss on her cheek. "What's up love, you look upset."

"I'm an idiot – I wasn't driving attentively enough – look what happened," she said, making a broad sweep with her arm towards the fender then bursting into tears.

"Oh!" he said, studying he damage. "Well, worse things could happen; nothing that can't be fixed at the panel beater." He took her into his warm embrace. "Not worth getting all upset about. At least you're ok, and I've booked for us to go to the local Thai resto for dinner, so that should cheer you up."

If only some of Richard's calm philosophical approach to life would rub off on her. Hell, maybe another twenty years together and it would. A glass half-full person could only hope.

Sharon Hurst

A flicker of time

Nothing in life is here for life.
Everyone and everything you see has a resting place.
Life itself is evanescent, and nothing lasts forever

Even the moments that feel eternal are a flicker of time,
a spec of your life.
We all have limited time,
But a myriad of opportunities,
And a limitless yearning to take them.
Every waking moment is a chance to take another step
forward.
Every handshake, every insight, every door you open is
a calling

There will come a time where the opportunities begin
to slow down. Everything seems to slow down with
them. Your body, the world around you, and time itself
slows right down.
This is how you know your time is running out. You
don't get to try again. So, it becomes time to reflect,
and remember.
You will remember everything- every achievement,
every smile, every laugh, every tear, every mistake,
every dream you made come true and every dream you
didn't.
Every path you walked, everything you're proud of,
everything that hurt.
You will remember it all

This is due for all of us.
Your time is limited-
What you do with it is not.
Bring every wish to life with what you have left, know
that your future is made of everything you do today,
And be unafraid to live the one life you have,
So even when time runs out, you can smile in pride,
forever

Maxim Anderson

Happy chicken

Yes, I was.

I was that happy chick. But once I overheard my Chick-a-dee sisters chirp on in a shushed cluck, heard them quack on about this shiny, clean, white-tiled place. They clucked on about its clicking pink lights, the clean-as-a-whistle shelves, the friendly beckoning windows into which all those very kind people who feed me peer in with cheer and bow.

What do they see? To what do they bow? This white-glazed hall of puckeringly masked faces is said to be where we, all the chickees, shall go. I wonder, is that the Heaven for chicks, perhaps? My sister birds say, we all end up there, all of us, and get a label stuck on us, (though I wonder, (being a rebel,) what part of us?) And if that's the 'Happy Chicken' badge?

To receive that 'Happy Chicken' logo, my fellow chicks tell a story, I have to confess, inconceivable to me – that my neck shall have to be wrung. Or slit. Or chopped off. That I shall only become that 'Happy Chicken' after my feathers are wrenched out of me, sometimes dead, at times alive. But, being plucked, it is said, is a tad better than the blades that chop and mince the baby chicks that have just stumbled out of their eggs. It is said, or rather, whispered, that my own ash grey dead flesh shall be injected with pink, the colour I'm assured, of happiness, which will tell the faces puckering and peering in the window that I was happy, yes, happy-clappy even to have my wings broken, my stomach slit, eviscerated, my guts fall out, and crushed. For then I shall be cut into 'Happy Chicken' nuggets and burghers and served up to children's delight. Thus displayed as a 'YUMMIE YUM!' I shall truly have been that once happy chick-a-dee! who ran under the sky, and pecked and frisked about, especially with my own little chick-a-dees each of them new, out of their eggs, the gifts of my body, now being shredded to be your chicken pie!

Bon Appetit, everyone!

Katherine Hoffman

Boss

The contempt in the words
smirk in the push
sneer in the pinch
and the sting in the slap

the possession in the bite
laughter in the boot
pressure on the neck
and the wallop of the punch

the control in the silence
the ultimatum in the bark
steel eye smiling,
ecstatic hand descending

every way, every day
poisonous patriarchy
at play

Sandra Lanteri

Outback

There's jubilation on the Diamantina
(I heard it on my bathroom radio)
For seven Biblical years it hasn't rained
But now over the flat and dusty plains
The flood-waters are roaring down,
Tsunami-like, making an inland sea.

Cattle have retreated to the high ground
To escape the rising water, and now stand
Belly-deep on their submerged islands.
Cattlemen in helicopter and jetski
Urge them into deeper water and back to land.

"Water is the lifeblood of the outback."
"They'll put on 2 – 3 kilos a day in this."
"Water is good for cattle, birds and tourists."
Life begins again on the Diamantina.

I switch the radio off, turn on the shower.

Anne Sedgley

Out of the hell-hole

Flaying, gagging, neck-slitting, stabbing, chocking, clubbing, crushed alive - the daily torture of millions of animals for the sake of human fun falls deaf on at least 90% of the 7 billion people on this planet.

Of course, it's a secret. Officially hidden from sight, there's hardly any awareness of it. Skedaddled past it by the law, shrugged off by the meat and fashion industry, ridiculed out of all conversations, buried under social conventions, it is absent from all public information and consciousness. And by the complicity of every one's silence. The absence of voice on this subject is imposed by the almightiest of social sticks, the one of custom, convention, tradition, all of it bolstered by the idol of personal pride, hauteur and habit.

This worldwide factor abroad on our entire planet could make any inferno superior to it.

And what makes the death of even the worst imaginable human scoundrel more bearable, is that most of us know, or have a strong feeling of what will happen to that villain after death. But there is no knowledge, scientific or religious – not even out of the mouth of a Jesus - of what will happen to an animal after a lifetime spent in horror.

The atrocity of global silence on animal affliction cries for an answer. The hell-hole routines of animal execution demands it. *Homo sapiens* is not the only specie. We are not alone on the planet. Animals are also alive. They are a part of us. How can there be meaning for humans, how equity, respect, or goodness without that? If the existence of animals is not defended, indeed, contained by a force of love above their own visible lives, then neither their or our own existence has truth or point, and would be perfectly silly at best, - not that 'best' or 'worst' in such a reality refers to a thing beside the passing sensations of victors. If some ultimate justice does not exist for animals, it will not exist for ourselves. Which would make life not awful, or bad, just hands-down silly, a chaos, irrelevant.

Katherine Hoffman

Remembering

I open curtains, let in light,

fling open doors, replenish air,

freshen far corners of my secret world,

soften stale crusts until they are palatable, feel words form, deepen love of trees and sky, renew each faltering step on a long snaking road, rekindle memories, indelible marks that life has left, illuminate small deeds that mean more than their parts, restore a shaky balance on the finest edge of a lengthy life, explore complexities of people close to me, of people that I know, that I knew; remember the woman who was my mother, her very being, her ideas, her laugh, her sadness, her voice, the give and take of her long life.

Ann Simic

The beautiful mermaid

The beautiful mermaid in the deep ocean looked sad.
The strong prince left her lonely, oh stupid lad!

How could you sacrifice your sacred love.
How could you treat your princess that tough.
She was such a magnificent piece of art.
She was an icon in loyalty, she had a pure heart.

Oh I know, you do not like the marine life.
Your royal family did not accept her as a wife.

Will you regret, will you feel guilty, will you be
shameful?
Will you scream, will you cry, oh listen it is not helpful.

The beautiful mermaid will move on and forget
your story.
She will finally find a courageous prince, so do not
worry.

Rahaf Al Maalouf

Are you still my friend?

Friendship is a two-sided sword
There is give and take without agenda
There is joy and pain without judgement
Are you still my friend?
When I speak from the heart it is real
What I expect is you to listen
I do not require fixing or advice
Are you still my friend?
When I cry, I expect compassion
I do not require that you agree, with
My way of doing or my conclusions
Are you still my friend?
When I laugh, I expect you to be happy for me
Even when my laughter does not make you happy
Even when you require something else
Are you still my friend?
When you tell me your truths, I will listen
When you tell me your pain, I will hurt
When you share your joys, I will be happy for you
Are you still my friend?
I will speak of my dreams
And ask nothing from you
I will share what I have, without dollars and cents
Are you still my friend?
If we share respect, I will love you forever
Walk through burning fires to protect you
Swim raging rivers to save you
Are you still my friend?
If you abuse my respect, I will hate you forever
Are you still my friend?

Peter Levy

Leaving

I'm at odds with my home town. I don't belong.

When I was young, my big twin brothers and I would, sit on the brick pillars of our front fence and play our travelling game. I would sit on the left. They would sit on the right. There was a division between us even then.

Our house is on the main road into town, and we can see the railway line clearly because of the footy oval opposite. The railway line runs along the base of the mountains that enclose our town. Ever since I can remember, these mountains have given me a feeling of being confined. I couldn't articulate it then, but I knew the railway line was an escape, leading to places I could only dream about.

As kids, we'd sit for hours waiting for a train to go by. Someday we'd be in one of them, taking us away. But over time, things changed, and I found myself more and more alone. My brothers, believing they were all grown up, said it was a stupid game only good for dreamy little kids like me. Then I got lucky. My best mate Sam joined me. We would sit there with an old globe of the world, twirling it, and as it slowed pointing to the countries we would visit.

I've lived in Yarrum, with my family, the Mc Duffs, all my life. Four generations of them. There's a saying here that the Mc Duffs are welded to the place. They never leave. Once, one did. His name was removed from the family bible, and never spoken of again.

Old Duncan Mc Duff, my great-great-grandfather, together with his six hot-headed sons, braved the high seas, and arrived early in Yarrum's history, and founded The Dawn Express, a small parochial newspaper with a pretentious name. It still remains the town's only paper.

Over the years, every birth, marriage, divorce and death, along with the town's gossip and scandals, have been documented by my family. It's almost our religion, this need to disclose the weaknesses of others. It is our family's power.

Ah, the arrogance of the judger. The duplicity of the trusting. We are the watchdogs of morality, with the skeletons in our cupboards shut tight. Tell the truth. Tell it as it is. The public has a right to know. Print it out loud no matter the outcome. Such was old Duncan's original dictum, which my father still dutifully follows. The town-folk choose to turn a blind eye on their and our mutual hypocrisies, for who else would supply the money for the footy clubhouse, and the free-flowing beer for all?

I grew up in Duncan's tall, dark, red brick house, with its rules and traditions. Built to his specifications, it looks too self-consciously grand for its environment. An embarrassment for me. Most of our neighbours live in sprawling old weatherboards, with verandas all round, for shade, and full of old sofas for sitting in, while drinking and talking with mates, with scruffy dogs at their feet.

Duncan's house is full of polished surfaces, tarnished silver and yellowing wax. Evidence of the pioneer making good in this new-old country. Mother tries her best to make it homely, but she has over a century of history to contend with. How can she get rid of the tears, and secrets caught in its corners, or the deep crevices of greed and intolerance that creep through the rooms, along with the cries of bloody stillbirths, tired old minds, and sibling rivalries? A family legend goes that after battering his young brother so viciously he lost an eye, Angus, the second of Duncan's hot-headed sons, was quietly banished, his name removed from the family bible.

I also grew up with the family's portraits hanging on the walls. Foxed faces, all marked with the same taut mouths, and high brows of belonging. Like branding irons. Top hatted, lace bonneted, bald, high bosomed, bespectacled, and long bearded. Great Uncle Edward, Great Aunt Catherine, Uncle Billy, cousin George. Mad, bad, sad, glad, pompous or indifferent. Very dead, they looked down on all of us, the living.

I have had to pass them every day. As children, on Sunday mornings before church, father would test us on our family history, and make us visit their graves in the local cemetery. I remember when I was about six, I asked about the space in between Granddad Sydney and Cousin Charles, and a clip over my ears was the reply. I learned not to question after that.

As I ran through the rooms, or slid down the bannisters, their boiled eyes would follow me. Glass blue. Mud green. Chocolate brown. But as I grew older, bolder, I thumbed my nose at them, stuck out my tongue. No bolt of thunder zapped me. No shadows climbed down from those walls to follow me. While my brothers revered them, and got caught up in the storytelling of them, I was more and more free of them.

By twelve, they ceased to impress me. They were the past. It was the beginning of my journey to claim my life as my own, with a new intensity.

At mealtimes, father sits at the head of the table, like some ancient lord, waiting to be served. Mother, nearly always in her uniform of tartan skirt, cashmere jumper, and pearls, summer or winter, sits at the other end, smiling.

Always smiling at him down the vast length of the over polished mahogany table. Hanging off his every word, which become hers, when she can remember them.

Dinner table talk is always small, insular, local. The outside world with its literature, philosophy, music and art, seems not to exist. At first, I tried to introduce these things but I was howled down. Being the youngest, I feel powerless, so now I stay silent. They take this as approval of our lives. Only sport, horse racing, fast cars and town gossip are talked about. Especially sport. At great length. Sport is God. Not to follow a team is unspeakable. Not to play even worst. We are expected to know our place in our family, and in our town. My brothers are content having their futures mapped out for them. They like being big fish in a small pond. They are puzzled why I'm at odds with this destiny.

As I entered my teens, the concept of what I wanted to be, to do, began to take shape. My schoolmates, Tom, Sam, Cam, and Lachie shared my thoughts. We wanted the autonomy to travel; to have more interesting lives that our conventional, narrow thinking town could provide. But time can change the shape of ideas, ideals, dreams, so that we can even forget what they once were.

Slowly I can see my mates are allowing other things to get in the way. I have watched them capitulate to the pressures from school, family, church, and now girlfriends. The patterns of these traditional institutions of control have gradually become harder to buck against. Their minds are already closing tight in denial whenever I try to discuss it with them. Their eyes and faces go blank, so I've stopped talking about our boyhood dreams. The distant lands they hungered for have grown more distant, the familiar home ground safer. Easier. All except Sam. He still needs to fly free.

However, last year, in the middle of a hard winter, Sam changed too. He became closed off. Somewhere else. He carried a pain he could not share with me. I can almost remember the time it started. I tried to help, but he shut me out. He became wild, angry, verbally and physically lashing out at everyone, everything. Then, as suddenly, he became quiet, sad and withdrawn. Somehow defeated. His essence had gone. I had my suspicions, but his parents said nothing. Then I noticed his uncle, my father's best mate, had quietly left town. There was no mention of it in the paper, and I was met with silence when I queried my father about it. It was just another example of his and the town's hypocrisy. More sweeping under the town's carpet of lies.

Three months ago, just before my nineteenth birthday, my father and I found Sam down by the lake. His favourite place where we'd swum as kids. With a rope around his neck. Still. I must admit it was not unexpected but actually the way of it, the seeing of it, rocked me. I can't blame him. I won't judge. It was his way of getting rid of the demons that tormented him. This town, with its indifference, its silence, and lack of support, had defeated him.

I begged my father not to report it as we had found him. Let it be an accident. Let Sam's family grieve in peace, with dignity. For the way of the telling will affect the lives of his family for generations. Perhaps forever. But my father would not capitulate. Only cowards kill themselves, he said. Compassion is nowhere to be found in his thinking. It was written up in the next day's editorial. Blind, patronising words about adolescence and suicide. About the youth of today. About their lack of backbone and character. About taking the easy way out. For all to read. Sam's young sister, Emily, refuses to leave the house, and a sad dullness has settled over the family. I visit them. Try to make amends, but I'm as damaged as they are. What can I really give them but my love? What to do now. Live with hypocrisy or leave. Then Emily found Sam's letter, written to me the day before he died, and I knew what to do.

Today is grey. Sombre. The threat of rain is there in the clouds. I lean out the train window and watch them. They are there on the platform, two small groups, awkward and apart. The old guard and the young, which really amounts to the same thing.

On the right, my parents. Father, all pinched lipped, and blind-eyed still. Mother hanging onto his arm. Bent. Small. Her real thoughts so deep down she cannot find them. And my brothers, bully arms crossed, legs apart, eyes puzzled. I expect it is only a matter of time before my name too is scratched from the family bible. And, just off to the left, Tom, Cam, and Lachie who once shared my dreams, and who have chosen to stay. Only Sam is missing, but he is in my heart, along with his final words to me.

As the train gathers speed, I watch them receding in the sudden rain. Hard, violent rain, washing away any lingering doubts to leave I might have had. Smaller and smaller they become as the ties of family, and old friends, stretch thinner and thinner until they finally snap, and I can't see them any more.

It's all so prosaic, my story. This story. Being told and re-told does not make the dilemma of the pilgrim less real. There will always be those who leave, seeking other truths. There will always be those who safely stay. Besides, Old Duncan did the same in leaving Scotland. Maybe I'm just completing the circle. My new clean canvas stretches before me, its future lines and colours an exciting mystery.

I close the window on my old life. And then the tears

come. Tears of exhilaration, and apprehension, and yes, I admit, some fear. I gather it all. Saviour the experience. And then I become at one with the train rushing boldly into an unknown life, in an unknown place.

The beauty, the history, and the wonders of the world are infinite, and fully unknowable, but there is the trying to see, to learn, to love and appreciate its mystery. To find my place in it, is my joy, my dream, and my challenge.

Sandra Lanteri

Contradictions

My life is full of contradictions
No single thing could ever define me
One day at a time is all I can manage
Pressure keeps me blind when I should see.
Questions of my past are always haunting
Reminding me of good and bad I've done
So easy to forget or change the details
To win the losing races I have run.
Underneath my world is empty
Victories are but few and far away
Whenever love comes knocking in the darkness
Younger hearts will always win the day.
Zealots live and die in silence
Always first to make their stand
Believing in the world the way they see it
Courageously committed to this land.

Peter Levy

My mother

When I was little, my mother
Taught me what love was.
Now, today, she is eighty
And still does.

When I was little, my mother
Wore a tight fair isle jumper with coloured stripes.
Her hair was gold, and one of her best hats
Balanced aslant on her head at a funny angle
Stuck on a hidden hatpin.

When I was little, my mother
Was always busy, always working,
Making the house clean, filling it
With flowers, sewing our clothes,
Our meals filled with carefully-studied nutrition.
(Is that why we are all so healthy now?)

When I was little, my mother
Split the kindling outside with a tomahawk,
Grumbling as she worked. This was man's work
And John was away somewhere with the army.
How I longed to be bigger, and strong and tall,
Able to swing the axe and chop it for her.

When I was little, my mother
Lit the chip heater through the hole, and left me
Under the shower with the flames roaring beside me
And I was all wet and bare.
So I screamed, and she came and wrapped me
In a big white towel, and it was all right.

When I was little, my mother
Heated the water in the copper with Ricketts Blue
And Silver Star Starch, and with the copperstick
Poked at the swirling shirts, popping
The ballooning shirts with the end of the copperstick.
I was allowed to push them into the mangle,
The wooden mangle that would have crushed my fingers
If I hadn't pulled them away.

When I was little, my mother
Was away for a long, long time.
When she came back she sat me
In a chair on the verandah,
Spread a white lambskin over my legs,
And gently laid a baby in my arms.
"Meet your little sister". I was very proud
But scared I might drop her.
Today she is my best friend.

When I was older, my mother
Gave my brother and me wooden fruit boxes
So we could build multi-storey
Cubbyhouses under the back tree.

When I was older, my brother and I
Dug great holes in the sand at the beach
And I crouched in them,
And Michael covered them with boards and sand.
We prayed for someone to walk over them.
But not my mother who was afraid for us.
She didn't know we were invincible.

When I was older, my mother
Was always busy, always working.
I wanted her to sit in a chair and listen.
I wanted to tell her everything, but she'd say,
"Follow me round, sweetheart. I have to vacuum,
But keep telling me." So I followed her
And kept on telling my story over the roaring and
Crashing of the vacuum cleaner, not knowing
How tyrannical the talk of a child can be.

When I was much older, she would tell us
In bewildering detail the minute life circumstances
Of someone she had just met. This used to baffle me.
Why should I be interested? I'd never met this person,
Never would. Sue, my sister, called this Mother's
Mrs Kafoops syndrome. "Did you ask her about x?" I'd
say.
"No," Sue said. "I meant to but she went on and on
About Mrs Kafoops, and I forgot."

Mother, you can go on about Mrs Kafoops to Sue and
me
As much as you like. We have learnt so much about
How to be a loving and lovely person
From hearing you talk about other people.
When I was little, my mother
Taught me what love was.
Now she is eighty
She still does.

Anne Sedgley

The Answer Part one

"They simply can. You simply can't. That's how it is.
That's how it will stay. Lay low. Stay down. Remain
where it's safe and comfortable, because you're not
suited for the world out there."

This is their answer.
Every voice, every perspective, everyone you know says
it

In your life, justice doesn't prevail.
Every path you take is barricaded,
And those around you seem to walk through the
threshold of impossibility like a breeze.
The rewards of life fall from the sky around them.
For you, every dream you've ever had was an imagined
story that can never come true

You turn and hide in your own shadow,
Learning to get away from the world because it didn't
welcome you.
Every attempt you made has lashed back at you and cut
deep,
You fell after every step you took.
They can all walk on water,
Because it's their world, made for them. Never for you

A small, quiet, empty space- welcome home.
Every movement you made out there was strenuous,
every back remained turned,
So you came here to stay because this is where they
told you to stay.
It's all part of their answer

The Answer Part two

The interface between the two worlds is both terrifying
and wonderful.
It is the line between staying where it's safe and going
where you haven't dared to.
A step back means remaining in the shallow water,
A step forward means you will be destined to a
burdensome fight

This is an unfair fight.
You will be fighting in a world not made for you,
And in this world everyone is praised except you- the
reputed inferior

The fight will be aeons of pain,
You will break and collapse and stare at defeat in its
blood red eyes and hear the voices say
"We warned you to stay out. This isn't what you were
made for. You can never win"
And this fight might have been needless; you could
have done what they said and stayed unharmed,
But for you the rewards of life must be earned

Your determination surges and your limits shatter,
You realise the only limits were in your mind.
You were born into a world where nothing can be
fulfilled without hardship,
But you will survive it, with an unbreakable grip on
hope, eyes that can see a future through the despair,
and somewhere deep inside you a voice crying out,
telling you everything those around you don't. People
say you can't make it, but you know you can.
That is The Answer
Maxim Anderson

A letter to vegans

"It's not about you, it's about your shout of "NO!"

If you're a Veg or a Vegan for your own precious 'me-centric' health reasons, then you go ahead, give this letter the flick, for it will be too big of an ask.

But if in that 'right-to-myself' health of yours there's just one shred of mercy for the atrocious suffering of animals besides your own say-nothing little dietary habit, you have to **do** something. You have to act. If you pity even the one animal out of the million who daily dies at the hand of 'Man', you have to stand up.

And shout a "**NO!**"

LOUD!

Vegetarians have to give animals a voice. They don't have one. Most humans can't hear their shrieks and gags and cries. If we don't give them Voice, we are accomplices to animal suffering.

So, why wouldn't you? The first thing I know, alas, from myself, is our refusal to shout that public "No!" It's a fear of losing face. A fear that your will be socially scowled at. Pooh-pooed. Laughed at. Ridiculed. Ignored. That if you make a noise, your social standing shall be impaired.

But how does that piece of gutless suck-up to conformity weigh against the horror of a lamb's slit neck?

You can also cop-out of the action by mincing reasonably, "My "NO!" won't stop the global slaughter".

Okay, that's right. But have <u>you</u> cried out your outrage to even 10 people of it? Haven't you even approved the slaughter regime by saying nothing at the party? The Barbeque? Or the dinner? By not expressing censure, indignation and yes, even the **wrath**, we concur. We are in neglect. Silence makes us complicit. That crime of vanity, it's a prat's pride, your not risking 'face' shall send an untold number of helpless innocents to unutterable affliction to die hideously every day. Our silence supports every one of those money systems organized around the right to murder creatures under the shibboleth of The Meat Industry.

So, what **can** you do? Here's the thing, it's so simple; when at table, shout that 'No!' Don't slink out of it by mumbling it, whispering, hissing, or allowing yourself even for a weasley, half of a second to feel shame or fear. Shout it, that 'No!' Go on, risk it, it's just your 'public face, it's imaginary anyhow, just a mask with which you're protecting - what - ?

Your reputation? Prestige? Other's opinion-of-you? Nothing else.

The way to stop the slaying of living creatures on the planet is by each person's clear and public shout of 'NO!' And stick to it. Don't let the public's stick whack the truth out of you. Just stay yourself.

Let there be one universal cry of 'No! at the dinner tables of the land! Because if in your private little life you're a Veg or Vegan, it's irrelevant.

*

As for all the God-faith religioned nicies, trotting home after Church of a Sunday for our roast lamb lunch, I ask; if this universe belongs to our God Creator, what exactly are we doing gobbling the flesh of the Creator' loved and living creatures? They belong to Him! They belong to themselves! To their own lives! Not to be our chops on our Sunday dinner plate. To believe that God can concur with any act of atrocious cruelty to a feeling being is the most heinous of possible mistakes with regard to God.

Just in passing, such violent disrespect for the Creation from believers, no wonder so many Aussies are atheists.

So no, please don't winkle out by meowing, 'It's not going to work.' We're not here for the reward. Or the pay off. Ours is the ACT. Don't count the costs like an el-cheapo scrooge or merchant. Just risk it. Walk it. Do it. Say it. Shout it! Do it and don't count what you're going to lose.

Alright, yes, that social loss, it really might be everything. So what? Surrender your booty of pride to that. Why not? The only purpose of pride is to lose it. Nothing else is going to do it.

Only your voice.

Katherine Hoffman

Assisi

Evening hangs slowly
In the misty valley
Below Assisi.

Up here the bells echo
In the little arches
Of the campanile.
The sisters bustle calmly for the cena.
Up the steep narrow streets
And out into the piazzas
The passegiata has begun to flow.

Shadow rises slowly
Like water
Up the rough pink walls and square tower
Of the castle, the great Rocca.

Birds wheel in the pink darkness
And settle. Shopkeepers
Take the plates and embroidery inside
Again. Soon, all will be eating.

Night settles around Assisi.

Anne Sedgley

The enlightened age

We are the enlightened age of a fucked evolution
No sooner believing and deceiving, we find ourselves
bled.
You walk over my face with some religion on nonsense
And I am still tormented, getting you into my bed.
Nothing changes quickly, prehistory in Plato's cave
Walking talking driving flying shitting skating fucking
Give me food and shelter baby, it's all I've ever wanted
from you
Stay with me tonight and let's watch the moon, forever
My needs are simple and I'll lie, cheat and steal to get
them
You strip me naked and console while I question
How can I tell you my feelings when I know you will
hear me
I want your body, in this time, for survival.
Bleed for me, breed for me, tell me you love me
Be nice to me, knowing my faults and accepting my way
Don't power trip me when you think there is pleasure
in it
Nothing means nothing, as my hair fades to grey.
Sometimes I see everything all so clearly
The bullshit to one side that floats through my head
A pain of existence that I know is universal
This life that we cling to, until we lie dead.

Peter Levy

The first Australian Outward-Bound School for girls

When my brother came back from a month at the Outward-Bound School on the Hawkesbury River looking brown and happy, I yearned to go there too. It didn't occur to me that he was happy because he was home.

There were warning signs. Yes, he'd had quite a good time, the other boys were a mixed bunch, the Warden, Mr. Deacock, didn't like him, he'd been Patrol Captain of Shackleton (wow!), he didn't like the Warden, his report said he'd done well in all activities but lacked commitment

He said they'd done bushwalking, canoeing, kayaking, ropes course, rock-climbing, abseiling, rowing and rafting.

It sounded wonderful. When I heard about the first ever Australian Outward-Bound School for Girls, I jumped at it. My parents agreed. And so I went. Plane to Sydney, train to Brooklyn over the steel-girder rail bridge and then motor launch up the Hawkesbury River to the OB School at Investiture Point. We lugged our bags up the hill to the dormitory hut, which was army-style fibro and corrugated iron on a concrete slab. Everything was army-style: the double bunks were iron, the blankets dark grey with a blue stripe. We learnt on the first day to do knife-edge hospital corners on our beds.

The Camp Warden was an ex-Women's Army officer who ran the school along military lines. Reveille was at 6 am – 0600 hours, they called it. No leisurely testing of the eyelids. By 6.15 we had to be up, toileted, dressed in bathers and sandshoes and out on some flat ground for calisthenics: jumping, stretching and toe-touching to blasts from an instructor's whistle.

Everything we did at the school we did in straight lines "at the double". After the calisthenics, we jogged down to the river and jostling at the edge in a cold cluster, one by one we entered the just-above-freezing water and waded across the pool to the other side. What would have happened if someone had broken ranks and actually swum, I do not know. The Hawkesbury here was estuarine, more salt water than fresh. It was a brownie-gold; you could see dark shapes moving in blurs under the surface. There was wire netting around the pool to keep out the stingrays and Port Jackson sharks, but it had big holes in it so we felt very exposed with our thin bathers and goosebump legs.

By now it was 0650 hours as we jogged back up to the huts to ablute. I don't recall any showers. But I remember the latrines. There was a row of toilets facing down the hill, partitioned off so you couldn't see your neighbour, but with no doors so the world could see you sitting there. Privacy was low on their priorities. I heard that for later Girls Outward Bound Schools they hung hessian across the toilets, but for us, as for all boys' schools, there we sat in a row, straining at stool. I went to the toilet in the bush whenever I could – not legal, but preferable to the latrines.

Back to the hut, make your bed, hospital corners, sweep the concrete floor, square off your pack, your chair and anything else. Now it was 0730 hours, Inspection Time. We lined up somewhere and points were taken off if your blanket's corners were puffy, or if there was fluff on the floor. You could lose points for your patrol for just about anything – not jogging when moving around the camp, for example. The central premise of the school was that you cared passionately about your patrol and its good name. The thought of losing points for Shackleton was supposed to drive me into a relentless jog.

Breakfast. Ravenous after our "swim" we poured into the Nissan hut and sat around trestle tables on benches, still in our patrols. All I remember about meals was a lack of conversation and trying to fill up on sliced white bread and butter, folded diagonally. I was always hungry at that camp.

After breakfast we jogged to Muster at 0900 hours on the parade ground. This was a beautiful grassy patch high up on the point, with a white flagpole on the edge above the river. We formed up in patrols on three sides of a square with the Commandant out the front, her back to the flagpole. We sang hymns, said prayers, heard notices and any punishments. I liked it. The place was beautiful. The flag was hoisted and I feel certain we sang God Save the Queen.

On the first morning we were told about the Honour System. At the end of the course we would each be awarded a Blue Peter badge: a blue flag with a white square in it, flown by ships in port to show they are outward bound. If any girl felt she did not deserve the Blue Peter, which signified full completion of the course, she was to say so. I wondered what this would do to girls with little self-confidence – an invitation to self-doubt and public self-abasement.

One last hymn and we about-turned and ran off up the hill to a big hut to do fitness tests. These were quite fun - up to a point. On Day 1 you did as many step-ups, star-jumps and other things as you could, and wrote down your pulse rate and how long it took to get back to its resting rate. At the end of the course, you did the same routines, took your pulse and compared the results with Day 1's. I don't remember my results on the last day – my mind was elsewhere; we were going home – but I was much fitter.

Chapter 2:   Patrols

We did everything in our patrols. My patrol was Shackleton, which had been my brother's – probably not by chance. In English boarding schools fifty years ago, they put brothers in the same boarding-house. Each patrol had six girls in it, except ours which had five. On long walks in the bush I used to imagine how good a 6th girl in Shackleton might have been – someone you could talk to, for a start.

The five girls in Shackleton were Jane, Jean, Eunice, Louise and me. We slept in two-level bunks beside each other, we ate next to each other, and all the outdoor activities were done together in our patrols. The idea was to weld us into a team. But it made for an intense loneliness if you were in Shackleton. I'd been made temporary Patrol Captain on the first day. Jean was Vice-Captain, Jane was Quartermaster, Eunice had health worries and Louise was never to be found.

Years later when I started work at the Victorian Correspondence School, someone asked me: "Which are you? Crook, crock or crank?" "What do you mean?" I asked. "Everyone here is one or the other – you don't get to be here by being normal."

The first Outward Bound School for Girls was just the same. Girls who were troublemakers or failures were sent there by their employers, their schools or their families, to be invigorated and straightened out by the Outward-Bound experience. The School advertised: "Send us your sick, your maimed, your problem girls, and we will make them whole." Only they used different words: character-building, initiative, leadership.

Shackleton was the archetypal patrol for problem girls. Jane was the worst. The minimum age for Outward Bound was 16 but Jane was just 15, she told me proudly. She had been expelled from school – she didn't say for what – and then they had relented: "Leave, or do the Outward-Bound course," they said. That made her my problem, though I didn't realize this at first.

Next was Eunice, a short plump girl with white skin and freckles and a pleasant, easygoing, dependable nature. She had asthma and was epileptic, and subject to crippling period pains. I think she had bad joints and a hacking cough. I could have liked Eunice, in a better world.

Jean was so colourless that I remember her now as transparent. Law-abiding, anxious, self-effacing – invisible. More an echo than a Vice-Captain.

And Louise? She was never there. It was cause for wonder that in a camp so strictly supervised, none of the staff realized that Louise's world gyrated around one thing – men. She was little and pretty, and could be helpless and vulnerable at will. She hardly spoke to us. One of the instructors was male – Andrew, good-looking, tall, expert at outdoor things – and where he was, there Louise was also. While we swept the hut and washed up after meals and did all the different duties of the camp, Louise was up at the back of the school hanging over the fence, watching Andrew work and chatting to him like a moth chatting up a candle.

Jane was determined to be Patrol Captain. She was always pointing out my imperfections: "Don't you know how to tie a sheepshank?" or dawdling so that Shackleton was last on the parade ground. I grew tired of fighting her malice, and went to see the Camp Commandant. "What is it?" she snapped. I felt like Oliver Twist. "Please miss, I don't want to be Patrol Captain any more. Jane Wilson would be a better Patrol Captain than me, and she wants to be it. Can I resign?"

"No, you cannot. I appoint Patrol Captains, not you or Jane Wilson. The fact that you don't want to be one is proof to me that you are the best person for the job. (The logic of this escaped me, then and now.) "Jane Wilson is a very troubled girl who has a long way to go before she is fit to be a leader. If she can be a good QM she'll be doing well. Now get back to the others. I don't want to hear any more of this." But the problem just went underground.

The heart of the school was the parade ground on the headland, looking out over the mighty Hawkesbury River, two miles wide at this point with about eight miles to go downstream before it flowed into the ocean. Next day we formed up into our lines on the parade ground, and the Commandant told us that all the knowledge and all the skills we were learning would prepare us for one thing: Fair Dinkum.

Fair Dinkum was an expedition we would do in our patrols, without instructors, in the final weeks of the camp. For 4 days and 4 nights we would go off into the wilderness on our own, canoeing, kayaking, navigating, camping, surviving. So they taught us navigation and first aid, how to pitch tents, treat snakebite and cook in camp. We were shown by a visiting District Nurse how to fold a nappy kite-style and pin it onto a shiny pink baby doll. Would we need this on Fair Dinkum? I wondered.

I discussed none of this with the other girls in Shackleton. Lots of absurd things happened around the camp, but I don't remember ever laughing. We were each shut up in our own cocoon of misery. We spoke only about the tasks in hand, and how to do them.

Every Sunday afternoon for two hours there was Quiet Time. For two hours you could wander restlessly around the camp, or sit and reflect, or visit the "chapel" (open space) on Holy Island. You could write letters or pray or meditate, but you could not speak. I wrote my most depressed and desperate letters at this time, praying my family and friends not to forget me, and telling them what it is to be so lonely that you ached, and stumbled when you walked.

My brother read these letters and vowed to visit me. He knew what it was like. He had said he might come on a trip to Sydney, and one day one of the staff gave me a message. "Your brother is at Brooklyn: he's coming up by boat." I couldn't eat, I couldn't talk or sit – I was going to see someone from home. It would put the world back together again, all the aching broken pieces. The hours dragged by.

Much later, I was called to the Camp Commandant's office. "Mr. Deacock tells me that one of your family tried to visit you today. It is a fundamental rule of Outward Bound that you have no contact at all with people from outside. Above all, no-one from your family. For the duration of the course. "

I could not speak. A huge pain was growing in my throat. "Mr. Deacock told your brother to go. He may not see you. That would undo all the good the school is beginning to do you in your development here."

They had sent him away. He had come all those hundreds of miles and they would not let him in. I said nothing. Right now, he was on the boat chugging back to Brooklyn, and I would not see him. And there were thousands of hours left of this hateful course which was devouring up my self, my whole identity. I turned and went out. I had learned to hate ….

Oddly enough, that had no connection with what happened in the bushes late next morning.

Chapter 3: Snake

The ropes course was slung between stringy-barks and banksias on flat open ground down by the river. It included a flying fox and a scramble net and various ropes to swarm up or wriggle out along. Like all the activities at the OB School, it would have been great fun to do with friends and was almost enjoyable, even with Shackleton.

Everything was timed with a stopwatch and had to be done at the double. The last task was to pitch a tent, blindfolded. This was practice for setting up camp at night in the pitch dark (so to speak). It was a glorious morning and with the blindfold on, I became very aware of the sun on my back as my fingers worked along the seams, looking for the ridge-line and the general shape of things.

I was having trouble with my tourniquet, a piece of plastic tubing that we all wore around our necks in case of snake bite. It dangled down in front of me and got mixed up with the tent-cloth as I worked. You lost points for your patrol if you didn't wear your tourniquet, or if you were found without your single-sided razor blade in your button-down shirt pocket. Snake bite treatment in 1960 no longer involved Condey's crystals, but we had been taught on Day 1 to cut into the bite to dispel the venom, first restricting the blood flow ("Release tourniquet every 20 minutes to prevent gangrene.") OK.

I was stretching out the tent guy in the darkness in the sun and thinking of lunch and of home, when the cry came: "Snake! Snake!" Everything stopped. It came again from behind us about 20 metres away. I pulled off my blindfold. Someone had fallen in the low scrub a little way up the slope and – horror! – I was the closest. Stumbling, and fumbling with my tourniquet, I ran over to the Camp Commandant who was flailing weakly in the scrub. "Where is it? Where?" I was wholly focused on the bite and the treatment I would have to perform on it. She pointed to her bare left arm. High up on the bicep were two small puncture marks across her arm, a little way below her rolled-up khaki sleeve.

With one hand I held her arm, with the other, my razor. Trembling but determined, I pulled the razor firmly across the two holes. The flesh opened in a white cleft, but there was no blood. "It has to bleed to get rid of the venom." I had no choice. Again my razor blade bit deeply down into the white cleft, and this time the blood came. The Major made no sound.

By now all of Shackleton and some others had gathered round to watch. "Get a stretcher" said someone and people rushed everywhere. The Major was lifted onto it and carried off, pale but brave. We all went to lunch.

Later we heard the motorboat taking her down to Brooklyn for medical attention. I was commended for swift action and (their favourite word) initiative. The Major did not reappear for several days, and someone else took the morning Musters at the flagpole above the river.

A rumour went round that the snake bite was a sham, a test to see whether we could cope with the dangers of Fair Dinkum. It was whispered that the fang marks were drawn on beforehand with biro. And this was true! I thought it was odd to get a snakebite so high on the arm.

When the Commandant came chugging back upriver,

her arm in a sling, an older and a quieter woman, we heard that "it had missed the artery by a whisker. She was lucky not to lose the arm." I felt confused about all this, but on the whole, not displeased.

Chapter 4: Skills for Fair Dinkum

The days passed, full of outdoor activities. One day we hiked to a great rock platform to see some Aboriginal art. The rock slab it was on was huge and dark, impressive under a clear blue sky, but all I remember now is my disappointment. A few lines, that was what all the fuss was about. In retrospect, I see that we couldn't hope to be fired up about a middle-aged white woman pointing out the art. We needed to be told the meaning of the rock drawings by an Aboriginal person. But this was 1960 and there were no indigenous people on bushcraft courses. This was before outdoor education started to take hold in private schools, and then to spread more widely.

In truth, there was very little bushcraft taught. The emphasis was all on skills and performance – on conquering the bush by surviving, not living in it and with it. Nothing was taught about plants, wildflowers, trees, birds, insects, spiders – nothing on bush food like berries or mountain pepper or mint or yam daisies. In those days, what you did in the bush, you achieved by strength, not by knowledge or experience.

The best things they taught us were the skills: navigation, map-reading, using a compass, and canoe craft, from two-person Canadian canoes to little flicky one-man kayaks. There were lots of rules about using these, of course:

No canoe or kayak may go off alone. Girls must stay in their patrols on the water at all times.

Girls must not sit on anything when paddling canoes or

kayaks. They must sit on the floor of the boat.

There must be no splashing, no ramming or charging, and no skylarking in the canoes and kayaks.

There must be no interference with other canoes and kayaks. Above all, there must be no tipping up of other people's boats.

After that, I need hardly tell you that canoeing was fun. We were always happy in the canoes, splashing, ramming, skylarking. Even Jean and Eunice found a tiny sliver of mischief, in the canoes. When the sun was out and glinting golden on the brown water, you could dig deep with one powerful stroke and glide soundlessly into the shade of overhanging trees on the bank. You could run a row of drips from the blade of your paddle in a line of bouncing droplets on the water. You could look down into the tea-coloured water and make out the dark shapes of stingrays on the bottom. There were quite a lot of them. We preferred not to capsize there.

But the best fun of all was sitting up high on our packs. The packs were army-issue dark-brown canvas sausage-bags tied at the top with a drawstring through eyelet-holes. We lashed them with rope onto wooden frames which had two straps (people, for the carrying-of). Although they ignored the sinuous shape of the human frame, and had no waist-belt to transfer weight to the hips and legs, they were better than they looked. Hip-belts were unheard of, then. You couldn't carry a lot in them, which helped keep the weight down; our living standards were pretty Spartan out on the track.

The best thing about these packs was their height in a canoe. You laid the frame along the floor of the boat and the sausage-bag lengthwise along it. Sitting up high on the pack, straddling it, you were a foot higher than usual and could paddle much more strongly, driving the paddle down into the water with your full weight, rather than across your body with arms only. You were much more unstable of course with your centre of gravity so much higher, so the practice was forbidden. But we made those canoes and kayaks fly across the brown water, learning not to wobble and flumping down off the rucksack to the floor, if an instructor came in sight.

The kayaks were one-person kayaks with a small hole for the paddler's torso. They could go faster than the Canadians, if you took risks. The trick here was to slide the frame in, stand the sausage-bag upright on the frame, and try to balance sitting on top and astride it while paddling. As your centre of gravity was up near the gunwale, this was very difficult and you fell in often, but it could be mastered in time.

They taught us how to keep the canoe heading straight by J-stroking, and how to raft up together for safety or companionship or to change crews and boats midstream. They showed us how to repair a canoe that was holed or damaged, how to do portages, and how to sleep under the canoes in heavy rain.

Once we were taken out rowing in a surfboat near the mouth of the Hawkesbury. That was hard work but interesting. I had seen Charlton Heston rowing a trireme in Ben Hur and would have loved a go at the sweep-oar, but that was apparently only for instructors.

Fair Dinkum was drawing near, but two good things happened first. One was being taught the basics of sailing in a gaff-rigged fishing-boat on the widest part of the Hawkesbury, downstream. That was fun.

The second thing was a visit by the legendary Betty Archdale, headmistress of Avonleigh Girls School in

Sydney. She talked to us about the usual things: courage, initiative, leadership, team spirit – but in a way that made them seem strong and real. As I listened, I visualized going up and asking if I could see her privately: telling her how lonely it was at Outward Bound, how full of high-falutin talk but cold and dim and critical. How it made you feel faceless and worthless, made you lose contact with who you used to be and full of doubt as to who you were now and did it matter anyway. I didn't go up to her, but I remember her warmly as the one rich and whole human being I met at Outward Bound.

Chapter 5: *Fair Dinkum*

There were six patrols, and all were going out on Fair Dinkum. The school's regime was designed to prevent any mixing between patrols. This partitioning reached its peak in the Seven Rules of Fair Dinkum:

No patrol shall join up with another.
No patrol shall take food from another.
No patrol shall take any maps from another.
No patrol shall camp near any other.
No patrol shall borrow equipment such as first aid kits and canoe repair kits from another.
No patrol shall speak to any person in the outside world, nor receive any help from any person in the outside world.
All patrols shall be self-sufficient and shall not eat any food or drink from the outside world.

Each patrol was set a different task on their four-day expedition. Ours was to paddle upstream a long way, leave the canoes and, using our maps and compasses, navigate to an old ruined farmhouse. We were to measure it up, describe and sketch it, mark it on our map so it could be found again, return to our canoes and paddle back to the school. I was disappointed on reading it. It seemed too sensible and straightforward for the grand culmination of the course, the famed and fearsome Fair Dinkum.

I was not reckoning on the sadistic spirit of the Camp, nor on the malevolence of Jane Wilson.

Our embarkation orders were clear:

Patrols will load gear into the boats half an hour before Departure Time.

Patrols will depart at 30-minute intervals in the following order:

Scott, Mawson, Amundsen, Shackleton, Evans, Cherry-Garrard.

All patrols will head off upstream. To catch the tide, Scott will embark at 0045 hours and will push off at 0100 hours.

Slack water is at 0600 hours, by which time all patrols will be at least 3 miles upstream. There will be some wind tonight and the moon will rise at 21:30 hours, so you'll have some light.

Quartermasters, fall out for issue of maps, first aid kits and canoe repair kits.

All others, to the dining hut for issue of food for 4 days' meals. At the double, go!

Each patrol had two Canadian canoes and one kayak. We wore an early version of a buoyancy jacket, bulky but not as cumbersome as a full life preserver. (Not as effective, either.) Each of us stuffed clothes, sleeping bag, primitive tent (two army ponchos joined) sandshoes and food into our sausage bags, collected the rucksack frames and life jackets, and piled them up beside our bunks. Lights out was early so we could get some sleep before setting off. I checked with Jane about our maps, first-aid kits and repair kits. She had put them in the boats so that was fine.

We were all excited about Fair Dinkum and the middle-of-the-night start down at the pontoons. After a few hours broken sleep, we put on our clothes, took the gear down to the pontoon and went back for our boats and paddles. It was very dark. The sky was full of heavy dark clouds, some with silvery edging where the moon was lurking. The wind was pushing up waves across the black water and they slapped loudly on the deck of the pontoon, making it hard to hold the laden canoes away from the edge.

All here? I checked the time on Eunice's watch. Gear check: packs, frames, paddles, buoyancy jackets, first aid kits, repair kits, maps, ropes, compass. As Jane confirmed each item, I ticked it off on my list. Everyone wearing their poncho? It looks like rain's coming. Time to go. Canadians first – give them a push off – thanks – paddling into the wind, out into the night. I was into the kayak first up and was surprised at the size of the waves and the growing strength of the wind.

The night was very dark. The moon had disappeared and the waves were thick and ridgy. Black water is much more menacing than green water by day. And the wind was rising. We could tell by the sound of it, a scowling roaring, and by the white foam that licked and vanished along the top edges of the waves.

We were heading directly into the wind and doing a rocking-horse dance up over the wave-tops and down into the troughs. We had come a long way out in the darkness and seemed to be handling it OK, but I thought we should raft up for safety, in case anyone was feeling scared.

Jean or Eunice could well be feeling unnerved. The lights of the school had long since gone out, and we were three canoes rocking and dodging about in the dark. Hard to believe there were other patrols out there somewhere. Rafting-up meant bringing the three canoes alongside each other, laying the paddles crosswise over them and holding onto the paddles and the edges of the canoes to keep the little raft of boats together. The paddlers in the outside canoes were responsible for keeping the raft heading into the waves. Like a trimaran, it was stable end-to-end but easily swamped. If a big wave caught it side on, it could be lifted and tumbled over, breaking into its three parts.

The wind had begun to howl now, and over to our right we saw lightning crack and heard the thunder growl. North could be anywhere. We could have been paddling in circles except for the direction of the waves.

"Jane, could I have a map and a compass", I shouted.

"No," she yelled back.

"Why not? I need them."

"Because I haven't got them."

"How come?" Something was stirring in me – anger, apprehension.

"Because I left them behind."

"You what? Why?"

"Because I wanted to."

"All the maps? All the compasses? Keep her head up to the wind, Jean."

"Yes. And all the 1st-aid kits and the canoe repair kits. Now see if you can do Fair Dinkum."

I had disliked Jane before. Now, out on the water, I loathed her. To prove her stupid, stupid point, she would not mind killing us all. We needed those maps.

There was nothing to do. Not even to figure out which was north. We had to survive this storm, get to the bank somewhere and then work out what to do. The wind was still rising and the waves by now were double the height of the canoes. The canoes creaked under the paddles athwart them and we had to take the waves diagonally, not front-on, to minimize the strain on the people holding them.

Big raindrops started to fall, bouncing off our ponchos and off the water beside us. If you ducked your chin to your chest, you could keep the rain off your eyeballs, but heading into the wind made it tricky. The outside people who were paddling were getting tired and very wet from excess water running down their paddles and along their arms. The inside people were tired from holding the raft together as it bounced and rocked. Changing places was out of the question: there was too much movement in the raft already.

How could we last out the storm? I passed around some chocolate and dried apricots to keep our blood sugar up, and suggested we keep warm by singing. No-one replied over the wind. So, I began to howl:

One man went to mow, went to mow a meadow,
One man and his dog, went to mow a meadow.
Two men went to mow ....

Eunice joined in. Jean might have or might not have. Louise was locked in her own world and Jane was just paddling and glowering, paddling and glowering ...

More rain, more paddling, more chocolate and always the wind. We sang all the songs I knew, and some of Jean's and Eunice's; we sang till we were croaky. There was water everywhere. Under the boats, in the boats, raindrops as big as pennies splashing in the water beside the boats. Our hair and faces were wet, and our hands and arms also, and our ponchos were just one layer in the general wetness.

At last, the sky looked lighter; the clouds were visible shapes. The night was dissolving. Where we had drifted to was anyone's guess, under the force of the wind, the waves, our random paddling and the tides. We knew if we paddled west away from the dawn, we would be heading up the Hawkesbury and must see a riverbank sooner or later. The waves were frighteningly high but the wind had dropped, so we could change places in the raft at last. Later, we broke into three separate boats again. I was still worrying about the lost maps and compasses when we saw one of the other patrols. By now we had a riverbank on our far left and knew we were travelling upriver as we had planned. We sat up on our packs and drove those paddles down and down hard, until we were in shouting distance.

"HEY!! WAIT!!"

Eventually, we caught up and rafted with them, panting.

"We're not supposed to join up," they said.

"We've lost all our maps and compasses", I said. They hardly knew us.

"How could you do that?"

"Left them behind. Complicated story. Can we borrow one of yours?"

Reluctantly they handed over a map, a compass and a canoe repair kit.

"Thanks awfully", we said, but Jane, who had paddled ahead in the kayak, said nothing.

"Good luck," we said to Mawson, who looked very disapproving. "Thanks again," and we paddled off. But they, like us, were exhausted from riding out the storm, and we ended up camping quite close to each other, further upstream. We slept all day next to our packs just where we fell – poleaxed.

That night someone from Mawson gave me some of her chocolate: mine had all gone in the storm. I realized that I had broken 5 of the 7 Rules of Fair Dinkum in the first 15 hours of the expedition.

Fair Dinkum was an anticlimax after the start. I had done harder bushwalks in Victoria. I think the others quite enjoyed it: we found the hut ruins, measured them up and sketched them. We camped our three nights out, dry and comfortable under our ponchos, and returned to where the canoes were half hidden, high up on the river bank.

But before we reached the river, two good things happened. We met up with an old farmer and his wife, a day's walk inland. We were short of water and very thirsty, so we asked them for some. They gave us water and invited us on to their wooden verandah, where they told us stories of the bush from long ago. They had lived there always and saw few people, so our arrival was a treat. As we weren't allowed to speak to any "outsiders", I did not record their stories in my log, and sadly I have forgotten them.

By the time we said goodbye we had had enough water but our food was almost gone. Then, half a day's walk down the track and in full sunlight we came across the orchard. It was fenced with barbed wire but easy to get into. Inside we threw off our packs and looked up. Above us were stone fruits, apricots, nectarines, peaches, ripe to the touch and juicy, as the birds had found. There were red apples, granny smiths, striped gravensteins and little crisp snow apples. The paling fence at the end had a passionfruit vine on it, and a pumpkin vine crawled about below. The old house was empty: the back verandah was bowing under a load of grapes in bunches. There were brown pears and green and yellow, and rows and rows of vegetables beyond the orchard.

We sat under those trees for a long blissful time. We hadn't eaten fresh fruit for days – or was it weeks? As we climbed out again, and I wiped the peach juice off my chin, one of the others said:

"Do you think it's stealing?"

"In Outward Bound terms it would be, so it's not going in the log. But we've left lots, and no-one could have enjoyed it all more, so no, I don't think so."

I felt happy for the first time during Outward Bound. The sun was shining, my tummy was full, I was not thirsty – a huge plus. We had done what we had to do, we were on our way back, and in a few days, I'd be going home.

When we got back to the school, the staff were at the pontoon to meet us, help us unload the canoes and carry them back up the hill. This was surprising. It never occurred to us that they had had no news of us since the storm, and couldn't know whether we would all come back.

This was nearly the end. One final ceremony down by the flagpole on Thingummy Point. We jogged down in our patrols, much more quickly than we had at the start of the course. We lined up in our three-sided square and the Major talked for a bit about how well we had done on Fair Dinkum. (Fair Bunkum).

Finally the crux: the awarding of the Blue Peter badges. Each person's name was read out, patrol by patrol. "Karen O'Halloran, step forward. Have you completed the Outward-Bound course satisfactorily, and kept at all times to the letter and the spirit of the Outward-Bound movement?" She would reply gravely or squeakily or with a snuffle, "I have". And the Major would lean forward and pin her Blue Peter badge to her shirt, and we all had to clap.

Patrol by patrol, till she came to Shackleton. I was first, as Patrol Captain. "Anne Sedgley, have you completed the Outward-Bound course satisfactorily, and kept at all times to the spirit of the Outward-Bound movement?" I saw us rafting up with Mawson, camping next to them and later, lying in the sun in the orchard, filled with nectarines and grapes. For a mad moment I contemplated confession. But I thought of how they had sent Michael back to Brooklyn, and how they had sent us out into that night and that storm, to survive if we could.

"I have." She had to pin the badge on me, no matter what she thought.

I held my breath when it was Jane's turn but she replied unhesitatingly and got her badge. Each of the others in Shackleton replied the same. Two-thirds of the way around the square, a girl whom nobody seemed to like stepped forward at her name call.

When she was asked was she worthy to wear the Blue Peter badge she said, very low: "No".

The Camp Commandant straightened up. "Why not?"

"Because I'm not worthy. Not worth it." We all stared.

Was this attention-seeking? No – she stood there, white-faced, staring past the Major over the river. This was a decision taken some time ago. No-one seemed to know what to do, although the whole ceremony pre-supposed something like this. "Very well. Fall into line," said the Major and moved on. What would happen to her? We thought she'd be taken off for intensive interrogation, at least. I don't think she was. As far as I knew, there was no attempt to understand her sense of failure or to combat it in any way. She left as she had come, unattractive, unpopular, and now a public failure, self-condemned.

In Shackleton we packed our bags: we were leaving in the motorboat in patrols. While we waited, we swapped addresses and phone numbers, and did the usual parting things. But I knew I'd never see any of them again. Louise had disappeared – we knew where she was. Finding her in time to catch the boat was not my worry anymore; I had slid out of being patrol captain like sliding out of a noose.

At last, with the afternoon sun glinting on the water as far as the eye could see, we stepped onto the boat and headed off down-river. We were homeward bound.

Anne Sedgley